Mocking Her

She turned to see a tall boy standing in the doorway. He was dressed in jeans rolled up at the cuffs. He had a long, rectangular face, with a jutting, stubborn jaw. He glared at her as if she had no business being in the beauty parlor waiting room. His hair was longish, and he had thick sideburns growing to the bottom of his earlobes. He definitely looked J-D, juvenile delinquent.

The boy sat down next to her.

"Do you work here, Miss?" he asked.

Amy shook her head. He had a low voice, speaking barely above a whisper.

"You here to get your hair done?"

Amy nodded.

"Do you have a voice?"

Amy looked up. The boy's blue eyes were crinkled up, mocking her.

**Other Point paperbacks
you will enjoy:**

After the Bomb
  by Gloria Miklowitz

Roses
  by Barbara Cohen

When We First Met
  by Norma Fox Mazer

Surviving
  by Elizabeth Faucher

Love Always, Blue
  by Mary Pope Osborne

The Ghosts of Departure Point
  by Eve Bunting

About the Author

Elizabeth Levy grew up in Buffalo and now lives in New York City. She has been a teacher, an editor, and a consultant. Among her many novels are *The Computer That Said Steal Me*, *A Different Twist*, and *The Tryouts*, all available as Scholastic paperbacks.

point™

ALL SHOOK UP

Elizabeth Levy

SCHOLASTIC INC.
New York Toronto London Auckland Sydney

Library of Congress Cataloging in Publication Data

Levy, Elizabeth.
All shook up.
Summary: In Tennessee in 1954, sixteen-year-old
Amy finds her life galvanized by romantic involve-
ment with a boy named Elvis Presley, who is just
beginning his career as a singer.
 1. Presley, Elvis, 1935–1977 — Juvenile fiction.
[1. Presley, Elvis, 1935–1977 — Fiction. 2. Singers
— Fiction. 3. Tennessee — Fiction] I. Title.
PZ7.L5827Al 1986   [Fic]   85–14328
ISBN 0-590-33115-9

12 11 10 9 8 7 6 5 4 3 2 1   1   6 7 8 9/8 0 1/9

DEDICATION:
Author's Note

This book has been a fantasy of mine for nearly thirty years. I, of course, am Amy. She never existed, except in my imagination, but Elvis is certainly real.

I first saw Elvis at Buffalo War Memorial Stadium in 1957. I think I was too self-conscious to scream. Instead I went home and told myself a story.

I was the girl who recognized something special in Elvis before he became famous. Because even then I was a good researcher, I fleshed out my fantasy with accurate details. This is my story. All the conversations and action of the story are fiction. All the conversations with Elvis are imaginary.

However, certain details are taken from Elvis' life. He did shop at Lansky's. He did graduate from Humes. Elvis had the courage to change the way he looked before he got famous. He had a sense of himself that couldn't be denied. He bought strange clothes at Lansky's when no other white boy would dress like that.

He knew that a barbershop would not be able to cut his hair the way he wanted, and so he went to a beauty parlor. I was not able to find out the name of the beauty parlor, and Easton's is a fictitious beauty parlor.

In 1954, he did go to Memphis Recording Service and Sun Records to find out what he sounded like. The receptionist there, Marion Keisker, thought there was something special in the way he sounded. Elvis paid his four dollars to make a record, and he thought it was worthless. But she made a copy and played it for her boss, Sam Phillips, who had told her, "If I could find myself a white boy who could sing like a Negro, I'd make a million."

A while later, Sam Phillips did call Elvis' upstairs neighbor, Rabbi Fruchter (Elvis did not have a phone), and the rest is history.

I want to thank Elvis for giving me such pleasure throughout the years. He opened my life to something spontaneous, sexy, and fun. He knew how to add life and soul to music, and most of all he knew how to move. Phil Everly credits Elvis as "the real advent of rock and roll." "He brought dance to the music," says Everly. "The entire world was feeling the beat. Presley just brought it on the stage. Thinking with your hips has always been popular."

I have loved rock and roll for nearly three decades now, but to me Elvis will always be special.

Chapter 1

"It's as easy to marry a rich man as a poor man," Amy's mother often said. Her own life made it clear that was a lie. Amy's father worked as a clerk in a drugstore. Amy had known, even when she was just a little child, that her mother's family considered her father a failure. "Alvin is just as sweet as can be, but he just doesn't have a business sense," went the family line.

Amy used to be embarrassed that her mother's relatives would talk about her father like that right in front of him. When she'd try to stick up for her father, he'd tell her it didn't hurt him. "Your mom came down to marry me," he said. "It was real love."

Amy wondered. If it was real love, wouldn't her mother have shut up?

Amy finished getting dressed, putting on a plaid wool skirt and a black sweater. Then she put on a strand of imitation pearls.

Her mother, dressed in a black suit and

high heels, her seams perfectly straight, looked at Amy approvingly.

"You look nice, dear." She touched Amy's hair, a delicate, fluttering touch. "You must tell Easton to give you a good trim. It's getting awfully long."

Amy's hair was cut in a short page boy, just below her ears. Amy wanted *really* long hair, hair so long that she could sit on it. But she knew what her mother thought of that. "Only hillbillies and crackers wear long hair and that's because they can't afford a hairdresser."

They drove together in Amy's car to Easton's, the hairdresser. Amy had gotten the car for her sixteenth birthday, a special, unexpected treat from her father. Even if it was a '48 Ford, six years old, Amy was still thrilled with it.

Amy's mother had the first appointment at Easton's. Amy sat down in Easton's waiting room, with its pink-and-gold-flecked wallpaper. She heard the bell ring on top of Easton's door.

She turned to see a tall boy standing in the doorway. He was dressed in jeans rolled up at the cuffs. He had a long, rectangular face, with a jutting, stubborn jaw. He glared at her as if she had no business being in the beauty parlor waiting room. His hair was longish, and he had thick sideburns growing to the bottom of his earlobes. He definitely looked J-D, juvenile delinquent.

Amy riffled through the pages of the issue

of *Seventeen* in her lap. She looked through the arch that separated the waiting room from the sinks and hair dryers. Her mother was under a hair dryer. Pink rollers in her mother's hair peeked out from the net at odd angles. She caught Amy's eyes and waved to her.

The boy sat down next to her.

"Do you work here, Miss?" he asked.

Amy shook her head. He had a low voice, speaking barely above a whisper.

"You here to get your hair done?"

Amy nodded.

"Do you have a voice?"

Amy looked up. The boy's blue eyes were crinkled up, mocking her. He had wide, full lips that curled up on one side.

"Sorry," muttered Amy, feeling like kicking herself. Why should she apologize?

"Why sorry?"

"It just slipped out. Forget it."

"Now I'm sorry, too."

"What are you sorry about?"

"I made you mad."

Amy stared at him. He was laughing at her. "I like your hair, just the way it is," he said. "I like the color of your nail polish, too. You don't look like you need an appointment at Easton's."

Amy stared down at the pearl pink nail-polish. She didn't know any boys who talked about nailpolish, for goodness' sake. Amy smiled at him.

Her hand automatically shot to her hair.

It was filthy. It hadn't been washed in a week, since her last hair appointment, and it was stiff from all the hair spray she had put on it to try to keep it in place. He had to be laughing at her. He was obviously some kind of weirdo. But what if he was really crazy? Amy could just see the headlines: "BERSERK IN BEAUTY PARLOR. Young Man Kills Mother and Daughter in Memphis Beauty Salon."

She stood up as if to stretch. She walked over to Easton. "Hi, honey," said Easton. "You look awful. As soon as I finish with this lady, I'll comb out your ma, and then I'm all yours. Don't be impatient."

"I'm not," whispered Amy. "It's just there's a guy out in the waiting room. He's weird."

Easton peered around the corner. "Oh him," he said cryptically.

"You know him?"

"Darling, don't worry your little head. I think he's just a high school boy."

"I'm a high school girl," Amy reminded him.

"See, you have something in common. Go sit down. I'll be with you in a minute. He won't bite you. I think he's rather sweet. He wants me to make him look like Tony Curtis." Easton giggled.

Mystified, Amy went back to the front.

"Satisfied that I'm not a murderer?" asked the boy. Amy noticed that he had picked up

Modern Screen from Easton's pile of magazines.

"I was just seeing how soon Easton could take me."

"Yeah, well I've got an eleven-thirty appointment."

"I didn't know that Easton did boys."

The boy studied the magazine in his lap. He showed her a picture of Tony Curtis. Curtis' black hair was curly in front, falling over his forehead, hair so greasy that it looked wet. The sides were slicked close to his scalp, but the back came together in a point at the base of his skull, each hair bluntly cut so it folded over the hairs in front of it into the infamous duck's ass — D-A.

Amy stared at Tony Curtis' picture. "Why did you come to a beauty parlor? Shouldn't you go to a barbershop?"

"Don't know any barbers who know how to do it right," mumbled the boy. At last he sounded embarrassed. Suddenly Amy felt sorry for him. Imagine a boy caring so much about his hair that he'd go to a beauty parlor.

"Does Easton know how?" Amy asked.

"I sure hope so," said the boy, and then they both laughed. "Did you see Tony Curtis in *City Across the River?*"

Amy nodded. It was one of her favorite pictures, the story about a Jewish gang in Brooklyn. The boys went to a vocational high school just like Amy's school; and just like Amy, Tony Curtis' parents thought he was too good for his school, until — by accident — their shop teacher got killed. Tony Curtis was good with his fists, but he was sweet, too.

Her mother hated the picture. It showed Jews in a bad light. Whoever heard of Jewish juvenile delinquents? She had wanted to storm out. Surprisingly, Amy's father had stood up to her and insisted that she could leave, but he and Amy were staying to the end. In the end her mother stayed.

"What's the matter with you? Didn't you like it?" asked the boy.

"Nothing's the matter with me."

"Well, you don't talk much."

"I was thinking about the movie," Amy said.

"Can't you tell me what you thought?"

"I liked the movie."

The boy looked disgusted.

"What's wrong? I told you I liked the movie. I liked it a lot." Why did he make her feel as if she was so bland? It was crazy!

"Okay." The boy laughed. "You liked the movie. I believe you. What are you gonna have done to your hair?"

"Just the usual. It looks pretty much the way you see it, except cleaner and nicer."

"It's nice. But you should consider growing it. You'd look beautiful in long, long hair, long enough to sit on it."

"My mom says that my hair is too fine to let grow."

The boy laughed again. He had a nice laugh. "Too fine . . . now that's a funny way of putting it." He started to hum to himself. "Your hair's too fine — "

"Too fine . . ." Amy chimed in with the harmony.

They started to giggle.

Just then Easton himself came over. Amy could never figure out if Easton dyed his own hair. It was a bright blond color that looked as if it came out of one of his bottles. He smiled down at Amy. "Well, I see you made a friend."

Amy sat up straight. "Are you ready for me?"

"Give me just a moment. I want to run out and get a cup of coffee, okay?" He gave Amy a wink. Amy wished he hadn't done that.

"Do you like Easton?" the boy asked.

"He's nice. Different. My mom and I come here every week at this time."

The boy whistled. "Every week. You must be rich."

"No . . . my mom just thinks that having our hair done is terribly important. Has Easton done your hair before?"

"Once, but he didn't get it quite right. This time I brought the picture."

"It really makes such a difference to you. Why?"

The boy shrugged. "Don't you care about how you look?"

"Yeah, but boys — "

The boy glared at her.

"Sorry." Amy wanted to change the subject fast. "Where do you go to high school?"

"I graduated. What are you — a freshman?"

"I'm a junior, at Humes."

The boy stared at her. "Humes! You look a little too high class for Humes."

Amy blushed. "No . . . I'm not. Besides, that's a mean thing to say."

"Well, I went to Humes and we didn't have no girls who dressed up like you on a Saturday morning. You look like you're going to a party."

"My mom likes me to look nice."

"Your mom looks out for you. She's right."

He confused Amy. Somehow she didn't like to hear him defending her mother. It made her uncomfortable. "When did you graduate?" she asked.

"Last year," he mumbled.

Amy was sorry that he had returned to mumbling. She liked him better when he was fast and funny. "It's strange that we didn't meet. I don't remember seeing you there."

"Yeah, well I was there all right."

Amy couldn't think of anything else to say to keep the conversation going, but she didn't want it to end.

Finally Easton came back and motioned for her to follow him. Amy stood up.

The boy smiled at her again. "Don't let him cut it too short," he said.

"Uh . . . look . . . I'm having a party tonight. Would you like to come? Maybe you'll know some of the kids."

10

The boy stared at her. Amy blushed. Girls weren't supposed to be forward. He would despise her. Why had she opened her mouth? But it was such a coincidence — meeting him on the very day she was having a party. And he had gone to Humes. They could have met.

The boy looked as if he was in shock. "Uh . . . thanks. I'm not sure I can come, but give me the address."

Amy gave him her address. "I don't even know your name."

"It's Elvis," he mumbled. "Elvis Presley."

Chapter 2

The faces of the men surrounding him were angry and ugly. His eyes flicked back and forth, searching the men's faces for just a glimmer of recognition that he was human. All he saw was hate.

"Don't touch me!" he screamed.

Suddenly, out of thin air, as if by magic, a thick, black chain appeared in his hand. He whirled it overhead, forcing the circling men to take a step backward; but still there were a dozen of them, and he was alone.

They laughed at him, standing clear of his chain, waiting like circling coyotes until he tired.

Finally he shouted two words at them, yelled them into the air. His tormentors disappeared.

He awoke, drenched in sweat. His mother was staring at him from across the living room.

He stared at her blankly.

"You were having one of your nightmares

again," she whispered in a frightened voice.

He still wasn't quite awake.

"You were screaming, 'Shut up,'" said his mother.

"I'm sorry," mumbled the boy.

"Don't be sorry. You weren't screaming shut up at me."

"I know, Ma. I'm fine."

His mother came closer to the couch that was his bed. The sheets were damp with sweat.

"Whad'ya dream this time?"

"It was the same, always the same. They were after me."

His mother nodded. "You okay, now?"

"I'm okay. Don't worry."

"I worry. Your father has nightmares, too. But at least he has them at night. You were screaming and it's just the afternoon, just a nap. Imagine if it were the dark of night. You and your father are quite the pair."

The boy knew all about his father's nightmares. Right after his father came back from the penitentiary, he would hear his father screaming in the night.

"Ma, I said don't worry."

His mother sighed. She kissed her son on the top of his head and then went back into her room.

Elvis stared after her. When she was gone, he went into the bathroom. He was dressed only in his jockey shorts. He looked into the mirror. The nightmare had mussed his hair. Carefully he combed it back.

"Your hair grows every which way," Easton had warned him. He had told Elvis to buy a little round tin of Royal Crown Pomade, a heavy yellow grease that the Negroes used.

Elvis thought about the girl at the beauty parlor. She had been pretty, but clearly she thought he was weird, weird to spend so much effort to get his hair just so.

Real boys were not supposed to go to beauty parlors.

Real boys were not supposed to wear pink and green. Those were pansy colors.

Real boys didn't have nightmares in the middle of the afternoon and wake up drenched in sweat.

But she had invited him to her party.

He reached for the little jar of pomade grease and put some on his hair, slicking down the hair on the sides. He put more on the front, on the part that he wanted to look curly. The grease made his dark blond hair darker, almost brunette. The light above the bathroom mirror shone down on his hair. He liked the way the light bounced back at him from the mirror.

Combing and fussing with his hair calmed him from his nightmare. He was less frightened.

He thought about those words he shouted: Shut up. He laughed softly to himself. In his dream those words had seemed magical, like an ancient, powerful chant.

But night after night, he had the same

dream. He was attacked by a mob of angry men, circling him, threatening as he hurled at them a defiant challenge, "Shut up!"

For no reason he thought about Amy, the girl at the beauty parlor. He liked the way she got dressed up just for a Saturday morning. It showed class. He liked the way she was a mixture of shyness and boldness. It had certainly been bold, almost forward, to invite him to her party without even knowing him.

He made his decision. He would go to her party. He'd see her again. And maybe again.

Chapter 3

Amy put on her red taffeta dress over her crinolines. She had to suck in her breath to button up the last buttons. She wished she had shoes with ankle straps. Her highest heels were conservative black pumps, but at least they were three inches high.

She wobbled down the stairs. It seemed unfair that she should be both short *and* uncoordinated. She longed to stroll languorously in her heels, her calf muscles tight. Instead, her ankles bent in like a child on her first pair of ice skates.

Her parents were in the kitchen. They had promised to keep out of the living room during the party.

"You look beautiful," said her mother, standing up. Even without heels, she was taller than Amy.

"Thanks, Mom. Now remember, no coming in and grinning at us." It was an old family joke, stemming from Amy's first boy-girl party in the seventh grade.

"Can you dance in those shoes?" asked her father.

"Of course she can," said her mother sharply.

Amy was grateful, but she wished her mother's voice didn't sound quite so sharp.

The doorbell rang. Amy hurried out to open the door, staggering a little in her high heels.

Carol and Steve arrived together. Carol was Amy's best friend, but she had been going with Steve for the past six months, and Amy had begun to feel like a third wheel. Not that Carol and Steve openly made her feel unwanted. On the contrary, Carol and Steve needed Amy to front for them. Carol's parents were dead set against her "going steady." Half the time that Carol and Steve had dates, Carol would lie to her parents and tell them she was seeing Amy. Amy found it romantic that her best friend's love life was being thwarted, almost like Romeo and Juliet.

Carol looked around Amy's basement "rec" room, suddenly making Amy feel as if the potato chips and pretzels were all wrong.

"What's the matter?" she asked.

"It's awfully light in here," said Carol, going around and turning off the light over the couch.

"Watch it," said Amy. "My parents are just in the kitchen."

Steve just smiled at her. "We're here to have a good time. Remember . . . for heaven's sake, we're allowed to turn off a few lights."

Carol laughed as if Steve had just made a wonderful joke. The other kids invited to the party arrived. Joey, Steve's best friend, came up to talk to Amy. Carol claimed that Joey was interested in Amy, and that Amy should be interested in Joey, who was going to college on a football scholarship. He and Amy were among the half dozen out of a class of five hundred who were going to college. But Amy couldn't make herself like Joey, and she suspected that Joey really wasn't attracted to her. It would be so convenient. He and Steve were best friends. She and Carol were best friends. A perfect square, but every time the four of them had tried being together, Amy had felt as if she was suffocating, claustrophobic.

Amy was popular. Amy had read about kids who were number one in their class and considered nerds. But that had never been her problem. She had always fit in, always been normal — even though she got good grades.

Carol and Steve began to dance. Their bodies were pressed together tightly. Carol's arms were around Steve's neck. Amy wondered if her parents would come out and see Carol necking and disapprove. Carol and Steve didn't even seem to care that nobody else was dancing. Amy twisted the glass of Coke in her hands.

The doorbell rang again.

Amy looked up. The boy from the beauty

parlor was there. He had actually taken her up on her invitation.

He was dressed in a bright blue shirt that looked like a girl's shirt — lacy flowers in a brocade, and tight cuffs at the wrist with three pearl buttons. He was wearing baggy black pants.

Most of the other boys were dressed in sports jackets and skinny ties and straight chinos. Nobody she knew would even consider wearing something like his outfit.

Carol and Steve stopped dancing and came over to her. Carol grabbed her arm. "Who's that?" she whispered.

"I met him today. He went to Humes." Amy left it deliberately ambiguous. She didn't have the courage to admit that she had met him at a beauty parlor.

"I've seen him. I remember seeing him in the halls. He dressed that way even then. He's weird," said Steve. "And he's dumb."

Amy felt a knot in her stomach. She stalked away from Carol and Steve, and went up to Elvis. He was glaring at her defiantly.

"Hi," said Amy.

He lowered his eyes. They were an extraordinary color of blue, and up close they didn't look defiant at all.

"I shouldn't have come," he said in a voice barely above a whisper.

"No, no," said Amy so quickly that she wasn't sure exactly why she was saying it.

His lips curled into the beginning of a smile. "You shouldn't have invited me."

"Why not? It's my party. I can invite who I want. Or, I guess it should be whom I want."

He laughed. "Yeah . . . whom."

"Would you like a Coke?"

"Thank you, Miss . . . yes."

Amy arched her eyebrows at the "Miss." "You don't have to be so formal. My name's Amy, remember?"

"I remember. Amy." He slurred the two syllables. Just hearing him say her name made the hairs on her arms stand up. She felt goose bumps. She lowered her eyes as she handed him a Coke.

"What do you do? Do you go to college?"

He laughed. "Do I look like a college boy?"

"I don't know what you look like. I've never seen anybody dressed like that."

"This shirt? It's stylish."

Amy giggled.

He glared at her.

"Don't be mad. It's just not a style I know."

"Then you don't know very much."

Amy looked into his eyes to see if he was teasing. He didn't seem to be. He sounded dead serious.

"I should leave," he said. "I don't belong here. I'll go."

"Don't." Amy whispered the word.

The boy smiled at her again. "Don't?"

Amy shook her head. She looked across the room. Carol and Steve were staring at her and then whispering to each other.

"Do you want to dance?" Amy asked.

20

"I don't dance," he said.

Amy couldn't believe it. How could he not dance? Everybody danced.

She held her arms out to him. "Come on," she said softly. "You can do it."

Chapter 4

Elvis wished he hadn't come. The truth was that he was a lousy dancer, and he knew it. When he stood in front of his mirror at home, he could move to the music. But when he had to stand in the correct position with a girl, he couldn't feel the music at all.

He looked across the room. He didn't like the people here. He knew they thought that he didn't belong.

He watched a couple dance. The girl had her arms high around the boy's neck, as if she was drowning and holding on. They were the same couple who had stared at him when Amy came over to talk. They clung to each other like two snakes humping, but what they were doing had nothing to do with the music. Every step they took was off the beat.

He glanced down at Amy. Easton had lacquered her hair so that it looked too stiff, but she looked vulnerable under all that puffed-out hair, her face tiny. Drops of perspiration were on her upper lip. She clearly was nervous around him.

But they laughed together. So few people knew when he was just funning. But Amy was smart. He didn't have to know that she got all A's to realize that. She wasn't just book smart, either. He could tell there was something about her that was special.

He pumped Amy's hand in time to the music, squeezing her fingers.

"Relax," said Amy.

"Whoever invented this position for dancing? It's torture."

"It's not so bad." Amy tried to fit her body closer to his.

She saw him looking across the room at Carol and Steve. She followed his glance. "They're in love."

"Every step they take is off the beat."

"They don't care," argued Amy.

"Would you dance like that?"

"Not that close with someone I don't know."

He stopped dancing. He wanted to slap her across the face. How dare she put him down? He squeezed her fingers hard.

"Did I say something wrong?" Amy pulled her hand from his. She rubbed the tips of her fingers.

He didn't answer her. Couldn't.

"You look so angry. What's wrong?"

He lifted his eyes. The perspiration was still on her lip. She must have felt him staring at it, for she quickly wiped it away with her hand.

Her eyes were deep, dark brown, almost black, and the whites were so white that they were like headlights put up too bright.

He willed himself to make his eyes look less hard and angry. Sometimes he felt so enraged he couldn't control himself. But he knew he had to. He knew that he could do it. He widened his eyes just a fraction of an inch, and then he lowered his head so that he was looking up at her, like a puppy dog's look when it knew it had peed on a carpet.

"Now what made you think I was mad?" he asked.

"How did I know? You looked like you wanted to kill me. And you shouldn't have looked that way. I didn't say I would never dance close with you. You just keep those glaring looks to yourself, mister. And don't give me that sad-eyes look. How come you manage to make me feel like I did something wrong? I didn't."

He laughed. She sounded like his mother when she was teasing him. "Truce?"

She held out her hand. He touched her fingers. They looked into each other's eyes. They both felt a little afraid, as if there were no secrets.

Suddenly Steve was standing in front of them, his feet wide apart. "Is he bothering you?" Steve asked.

"Are you crazy?" whispered Amy. "He's not bothering me."

"Carol heard you fighting," said Steve. "She was worried."

"Just buzz off," said Amy, reaching for Elvis' hand. She was surprised to feel it clammy and wet with sweat.

Elvis didn't look up. His eyes stayed hooded as if he were studying the linoleum pattern between Steve's wide-planted feet. He ground his teeth in the back of his jaw together. He could feel the sweat under his armpits. He knew that Amy's friend was looking for a fight. Amy didn't realize it. She thought she could just tell him to buzz off. He wouldn't. He wanted to fight.

Elvis *hated* to fight. He was scared of fighting, had been back when he was a little boy, and he had never outgrown it. When he was little he had been accused of being a mama's boy. Truth was, his mama had always tried to protect him, always told him not to fight, but to run to her. He was different, she said. He wasn't like other boys, and he shouldn't let them beat him up, just because he was different. Even in high school, when he was a freshman, when he was way too big, she used to walk him to school just so that he wouldn't get into fights with other boys.

Elvis had learned to smell when a fight was coming. He didn't know why guys liked to beat up on him so much; he just knew they did. He could tell from this guy's tone of voice — Steve wanted to beat him up. He would beat him up.

"I said to buzz off," repeated Amy, her voice unnaturally high. "He's not bothering me."

"You sure? We don't like crashers. We don't like greasers."

"Steve . . . it's my party. I invited him."

Steve stared at her as if he was sure she was lying.

Joey stood next to Steve. "What's going on?" he asked, glaring at Elvis.

Steve smiled. "I just wanted to make sure Amy was all right."

"I'm fine. He's a friend of mine."

The party had come to a dead stop. All the kids stood around, staring at Elvis. "Can you believe this guy's hair?" Joey said to Steve.

"That must be one of those duck's asses."

"He sure looks like a duck's ass. Probably smells like one, too." Joey shoved Elvis hard, pushing him in the chest. Elvis backed up a step and landed on the couch.

"Suppose your mother's a duck, too," sneered Joey, keeping his voice playful.

"I guess that makes his father a mother-duck," said Steve with a laugh.

"Probably doesn't have a father," added Joey.

"Cut it out!" yelled Amy. "Both of you. Why don't you guys just shut up!" She turned to Elvis and said, "They're just smart asses. Don't pay any attention to them."

"What's the matter, duck's ass? Cat got your tongue?"

Elvis started to get up off the couch, and Steve leaned over, putting his hands on Elvis' shoulder, and pushed him back down.

"Where are you going, duck's ass? We're just beginning to have fun."

Amy stomped between them. "Get out of here, you morons! Get out of here, or I'll get my dad to kick you out." Slowly and reluctantly Elvis stood up behind her.

The boys paid no attention to her. Joey pushed her aside, and then shoved Elvis down harder. He landed on the couch. He started to get up again, and once again was shoved down, but this time, finally, on the way down, he took a swing, but he could get no leverage, trying to swing when he was falling down. His blow glanced off Steve's shoulder.

Amy screamed, "Stop it!"

Steve and Joey jumped on top of Elvis on the couch.

Elvis turned into a ball. Steve and Joey kept punching him, flailing at him. He felt the fists thumping his ears, stinging sharply. He wanted it to be like his dream, but no magic black chain appeared. He whispered, "Shut up," but nobody heard him.

Steve twisted the back of Elvis' shirt, so that it was getting tighter and tighter against his neck. He was choking. He tried to wiggle free. He kicked out with his feet.

"Oh, lookee, lookee . . . the fairy's fighting back. Get on your feet, you faggot. Fight like a man."

Elvis struggled for air, coughing and choking. He bit his tongue, and he could feel blood in the back of his mouth.

"Amy, help!" he whispered. "Help!"

He felt tears in the corners of his eyes. As if from a distance, he heard Amy yelling, "Help!"

Then he heard an adult voice shouting, "What the hell's going on here!" Amy's father stormed into the room, grabbing Joey and Steve by the back of the neck. "What's the matter with you jerks? What are you beating up on this guy for? You okay, kid?"

Elvis looked down at himself. His favorite blue shirt was torn. His ears and his forehead were red. He squinted to try to keep back the tears.

"Yes, sir, I'm okay."

Amy's father turned to the kids on the floor. "Steve, you and Joey get out of here. You oughta know better. Bad enough two on one, but this kid's barely one. You guys oughta save it for the football field."

"Gee, Mr. Klinger. He started it. He swung at us."

Amy's father sort of winked at them. "Yeah, I'm sure."

Joey and Steve started to grin.

"They started it," shouted Amy. "Elvis wasn't doing anything."

Her father sighed. "Amy, it doesn't matter who started it. Your mother and I do not allow fights in our house. Anyhow, it's getting late. You kids oughta be leaving. I think the party's over."

Amy's father helped Elvis up. "Kid, why don't you go clean up."

Elvis started to walk to the bathroom, his

head hanging. Carol came up to Amy. "Are you okay? Do you want me to stay?"

Amy shook her head. She could barely talk. She hated Joey and Steve for ruining her party, for beating up on Elvis just because he wore his hair different and looked different.

Joey and Steve started to put on their coats to leave. As they left, they turned to Elvis. "See you around, D-A . . . soon."

Amy waited until Elvis was in the bathroom. Then she turned on Joey. "Don't you ever touch him again," she hissed. "You do and I'll personally write bully across your forehead in indelible ink. Now get out of here."

"Whoa," said Joey. "You prefer him to me?"

"You've got it," snapped Amy. "In a nutshell, which is about the size of your brain."

"Hey, wait a minute," said Joey. "Nobody talks to me like that. Even Miss Grade A . . . A . . . for — "

Carol took Joey's arm. "Come on," she said. "Everybody's upset. Let's go. Amy, I'll talk to you tomorrow."

Amy watched them leave. Her friends, she thought. Some friends. She waited for Elvis to come out of the bathroom.

Chapter 5

Elvis came out of the bathroom, rubbing his cheek. Amy was putting records away. She looked as if she wanted to cry.

"I'm sorry I ruined your party," he said.

She shook her head. "It wasn't your fault."

He laughed. He knew whose fault it was. Of course, it was his fault. Who else?

"Why are you laughing?" she asked.

"Sorry."

"Don't be sorry. But — "

He could tell that she was going to start bawling at any moment. "Don't cry."

"I'm not going to cry. I'm mad. And not at you. You didn't do anything wrong. You're the one who got beat up. It was awful. I'm so sorry. Steve and Joey shouldn't have done that."

He shrugged. He knew why they had done it. He knew they thought he was asking for it.

"Don't you even care that they beat you up?"

"I care. Don't worry about that. Where's your father?" he asked nervously. He looked around the basement rec room, as if seeing it for the first time, the blond plywood papered over to look like wood paneling. There was even a pinball machine in the corner.

"He's upstairs. The party's over. I guess that's obvious."

"I'd better go, too."

She nodded, but she looked so sad that he wanted to take her into his arms and make everything all right for her.

"Someday I'll make it up to you," he said. "I'll give you a party that nobody will ever forget."

She laughed. "I don't need a party. I just had one. The last thing I need is another party."

"You're going to get a better one, anyhow. I'll give you one when you go to college. I've never known a college girl."

"*If* I go it won't be such a big deal. I'll only go to Tennessee State if I get a scholarship. It's only a big deal at Humes. Anywhere else it would be small potatoes. My cousin is going to Tulane in New Orleans. Now that's a big deal. But I won't be going to college at all if I don't get a scholarship. My parents can't afford it."

"Stop putting your parents down." His voice was low, but it made her shut up. "I don't like it when you talk like that. You shouldn't talk like that about your family.

31

Your daddy certainly cares for you. And I bet it's not so easy on him, sending you to college, scholarship or not. You shouldn't put your parents down."

"I'm not putting them down."

"You're putting down your family. I don't like it. I don't like girls who do that."

"Okay, okay, don't yell at me. You sure don't have trouble telling me off. I wish you had told off Joey and Steve." She sat down on the sofa. "You're weird, you know that?"

He shrugged, that peculiar shrug that she had noticed in the beauty parlor. "I'm not so weird," he said, his voice so soft now that she could barely hear it, but the voice seemed to carry an implied threat with it.

She played with the hem of her dress nervously. "You are," she whispered back. "But I'm not so sure weird is bad."

He laughed out loud, almost a hoot, covering up his mouth as he laughed as if he had bad teeth, but he didn't. His teeth were white and straight.

She laughed with him, although she wasn't completely sure exactly why she was laughing. He gave her a slow grin. She wondered how anybody could resist that smile.

Amy searched for something to say . . . anything to prolong the moment. "You sure you weren't hurt?"

"Sure . . . don't worry about me."

"They made me so mad. I told them off."

"I heard you. I shouldn't let a girl fight my battles. Someday I'll teach them."

"Don't do anything stupid. Joey's pretty strong."

"You saying I'm weak?"

"No . . . no . . . don't get that snapping-turtle look."

He was so surprised by her words that he threw back his head and laughed. "Snapping turtle?"

"Well, that's just what you look like when you get all ornery. I don't like it. I'm not picking a fight with you."

"I know," he said softly.

She paused. She picked up one of his hands and touched it gently. "Why do you dress so differently if you don't want to get beat up?"

"Why should they want to beat me up just 'cause they don't like the way I look? It's a free country. I just want to look like this. Is that bad?"

Amy shook her head. "I feel different inside, too, but I don't show it to everybody."

"I don't feel different inside. This is just the way I like to look." He set his jaw stubbornly.

Amy kept hold of his hand. His moods seemed to shift so often. She couldn't keep up with them.

She stroked his hand again. He relaxed. "I'm glad you came," she said.

He laughed. "Yeah, I ruined your party and I got beat up. A great night."

"But we're together."

He looked at her, but he didn't make a move to kiss her. Amy wished that he would.

Instead he pulled his hand away. "I should be going."

"Okay."

Just then she saw her father's head appear in the basement doorway.

"Amy?"

"Yes, Dad."

"What are you doing down there?"

"Just talking."

"Your party's over."

Her father took the stairs two at a time. He seemed to fill the entire doorway. He glared at Elvis. "You're still here."

Elvis lowered his head again. "Yes, sir, I am." He was mumbling now; all traces of the funny guy who had told Amy not to put her family down were gone. He was now nothing but a super-polite mumbler.

"Dad, he's leaving. I'll walk him out."

"You'll stay here," said her father. "He can walk himself out. Can't you, son?"

Elvis heard the sneer in the man's voice, the fact that he obviously thought that Elvis was a sissy, not good enough for his daughter. Amy's father would have preferred a kid who would have fought back, not one who cowered in the corner of the couch with tears in his eyes, certainly not one who met his daughter in a beauty parlor.

Elvis stood up. He was nearly six feet tall, but he was so slim that he seemed small compared to Amy's father who was the same height, but built like a bowling pin.

"Amy, thanks for having me. I'll be seeing you."

"Wait a minute," said her father menacingly. "What do you mean, I'll be seeing you?"

"Nothing, sir."

"You will not be seeing my daughter. I want to make that clear."

"Daddy!"

"Well, we might as well get that settled right now. I don't want you seeing this boy. It's not right."

"What do you mean, it's not right? You can't tell me who I'll see or won't."

"Of course, I can," snapped her father. "Who else has the right? I'm sorry, young man, but I don't want to say anything behind your back that I won't say to your face. I'm not that kind of a man. But I'll be honest with you. I don't want to see you around here."

"Why, sir?" The lip curled up for just a second, not seriously, but enough to let both Amy and her father see that the "sir" should not be taken too seriously.

"Because I don't like your manner. We don't know you. And I don't like what happened here."

"It wasn't his fault!" Amy's voice was shrill.

"Where do you go to school?" Amy's father asked.

"I graduated from Humes last year. I've got a job. I drive a truck for Crown."

Amy's father seemed to consider this news, trying to find something in it worthy of forbidding him to see Amy. "Boy, is somebody making you wear your hair like that?"

Elvis shook his head from side to side.

"I rest my case," said Amy's father. He turned on his heel and walked up the stairs.

"Amy, say good-bye." She watched her father climb the stairs.

"I guess you'd better go," said Amy.

"I know." But Elvis made no move to get up and leave.

Amy put her hand on his shirt. "I'm going to see you again," said Amy.

He shook his head. "I don't know . . ." he mumbled. "I don't want to get your father mad."

Amy reached up and kissed him on the cheek. "It's me he'll be mad at — not you. He can't tell me who I can see or not. Besides, he's just upset because of the fight. I'll talk to him later."

Elvis smiled. "I think it's crazy."

"Is it crazy for me to like you?" Amy asked.

Elvis smiled again. "Yeah, I think maybe it is."

Chapter 6

On Monday, at school, Carol cornered Amy outside on the wide walk that led to the huge red brick building. "Amy, I've got to talk to you."

Amy hugged her books to her chest as if they were a shield. "Sorry my party was such a disaster," she mumbled into her history text.

"What made you invite that creep to your party?" Carol asked.

"I don't think he's a creep."

"Are you kidding? He lives near the projects."

"What difference does that make? He's got a job driving a truck."

Carol studied Amy as if she were crazy. "A truck driver. For you, Amy Klinger? The girl who's going to college? Think about his looks."

"I think he's cute."

"Cute! He's the ickiest guy I've ever seen. He's a greaser, and he's a sissy."

"He's not a sissy."

"Oh, yeah? Then why did he let Steve beat up on him like that?"

"Why do you think Steve wanted to beat up on him?"

Carol stopped.

Amy swallowed hard. She knew Carol would not be able to answer her question.

"Look, Amy . . . I think you'd better do some thinking about who your friends are. I mean it."

Amy laughed. "Carol, will you stop taking everything so seriously? That sounds like a line from a bad Western."

Carol looked a little bit ashamed of herself. "Come on," said Amy, grinning. She knew she had the advantage for a second. "We'll be late for class."

Amy skipped up the stairs to school, saying hello to kids as she passed them. Kids came up and wanted to talk about the fight at her party. It hadn't been a boring party. No matter what else had happened that night, it hadn't been boring — thanks to Elvis.

Amy made her way through the corridor, carrying her usual load of books. The big black notebook filled with painstakingly written notes formed the base of the triangle. The heavy history book came next, then the chemistry text with its complicated picture of an atom, and at the pinnacle a small French book balanced precariously.

The armor of a grade-A student. Everyone thought that good grades just came naturally to Amy. She knew that she worked for them, worked hard, for her only hope of getting away to college would be if she won a scholarship. More than anything else, Amy wanted to get away, far away.

At the end of the day Amy walked out of the Gothic-arched doorway of Humes and saw Elvis waiting for her, standing by a pickup truck.

She hurried down to the curb, smiling. He was the smallest tall boy she had ever seen. His hips were so slim they looked as if they could break. Only his arms looked rounded, almost baby fat on his elbows.

He gave Amy a slow grin.

"Hi," she said, her voice somehow sounding much more breathy than normal, as if she were trying to imitate Marilyn Monroe. "I didn't expect to see you," she said.

"I had a delivery around here. I thought I'd see if you'd be getting out of school." He looked down at her pile of books. "You weight-lifting?" he asked.

Amy giggled as if he had just made a brilliant remark.

"No . . . that's my normal load. I'm taking the Regents."

He nodded. Girls like her always carried a huge pile of books around, as if they ran the world. But he liked her.

"You really going to be a college girl?"

"Yeah, didn't you believe me the other night? You make it sound like a disaster."

"Naw . . . that's good for you."

"But not for you."

He laughed, an almost crazy laugh. "Yeah, can't you see me as a college boy?"

"It's a free country. Everybody's got a chance to be whatever they want to be."

He looked down at her. She knew he was laughing at her. "Don't you believe anybody can be whatever they want?" Amy insisted.

"Oh sure, that's why I get beat up just because I get a haircut that I like."

"Why do you have to be so different? I mean, I like your hair, but if it gets you in such trouble . . . why bother?"

He didn't answer her. He shifted uncomfortably. "You want to go for a ride?" he said. "I'll drop you home."

"I'd like to, but I got my car."

He held his head down. "You have a car?"

Amy nodded her head. "It's a beat-up Phaeton, but my father gave it to me when I was sixteen. He said that if I were a boy, he had planned on giving his son a car when he was sixteen; and since my ma couldn't have any more kids, the one thing he wanted me to have was a car."

"It must be nice being rich."

"We're not rich. We're poor."

He laughed at her as if she had just made the best joke in the world. "You poor! You got a house. You got a car." He wiped away tears from his eyes, he was laughing so hard.

She blushed. "But we're poor compared to my mom's family. They've got lots of money."

"Believe me, you're not poor."

"Well, you don't have to go on about it," she said huffily. "Why did you come to see me today?"

"I shouldn't have," he said angrily.

Amy stared at him. "What's wrong with you?" she asked. "You don't make a date, you just show up after school without telling me, and then you act as if I did something wrong."

"Your father said you weren't supposed to see me."

"I know, but I want to."

"I don't want your father mad at me."

"It's me he'll be mad at, not you."

He shook his head at her. "Girl, why are you so crazy?"

"Nobody who knows me thinks I'm crazy. I'm known as a very sane person."

"Then you don't belong with me."

Amy wanted to hit him. "Why are you making this so difficult?"

"Because it was a mistake to come see you."

For a second there was such fury on his face that Amy was almost afraid. He was weird, all right, too weird.

Elvis turned on his heel and stepped up into his truck.

"Elvis," demanded Amy, "what's going on? Where are you going?"

"I've got work to do, college girl. Not like you."

"I'm not a college girl yet. You're the one who came to see me."

"I told you it was a mistake." He started the engine and peeled away. He didn't need her. He didn't need anyone.

Carol came and stood next to Amy. "What was that all about?" she asked.

Amy shook her head. "I haven't the foggiest idea. He came to see me and then he got mad."

Carol sighed. "Amy, listen, take my advice. You two have nothing in common. It'll be better if you never see him again."

"Yeah," said Amy. But she didn't believe it. He was like someone out of control. He was polite one minute and crazy the next. But deep inside, Amy felt the same way. She just hoped that Elvis wasn't out of her life forever.

Chapter 7

Elvis was embarrassed, embarrassed by how he had behaved — showing up at his old school like a love-sick cow. He was mad at himself for thinking about Amy so much. But he couldn't get her out of his mind.

It was Saturday. He hadn't seen her or called since Monday. He knew she'd be at Easton's. She said she went every Saturday with her mother. Could he claim that he needed a haircut again? That would give him an excuse to see her. He studied himself in the mirror, carefully putting on the Royal Crown Pomade. He didn't really need a haircut, but perhaps he could go and pretend that he had a question for Easton.

He looked at his watch. It was only nine-thirty in the morning. Amy wouldn't arrive at Easton's until eleven.

Slowly Elvis got dressed. He pulled up the collar of his plaid shirt, but the green and blues of the shirt were wrong.

He looked at the drawer and riffled through

the shirts there. None of them seemed right. He needed something special. Perhaps if he had something new he'd feel better. If he was wearing something new he could go see Amy at Easton's, and everything would start anew.

He combed his hair again, smoothing it down each time until the palm of his hand was covered with grease.

In the corner of his mirror he saw his mother, staring at him. "Is anything wrong, Ma?" he asked.

She shook her head. She came and sat on the edge of his bed. "Your pa's feeling bad again. He's too sick to go to work."

Elvis didn't answer. He just kept combing his hair. But he felt his stomach muscles tighten. He gave his mother his whole paycheck, every week. His mother then doled out money to him when he needed it. Fifty cents or a dollar for a date. No more. They barely had enough as it was, especially with his daddy sick so much. His father was always calling in sick — not that his father was a drunk, like some, he was just sickly.

"Your hair looks nice," said his mother with a giggle. "You've got that look in your eye. You've got a girl, don't you?"

He turned and gave his mother a slow smile. "You're my best gal."

"But you've got another one."

He shook his head.

"Don't lie to me. A mother can tell. It's not a sin. Is she a nice girl?"

"She's 'uptown.'"

His mother bristled like a small animal, trying to make itself look bigger than it was by pushing up its small hairs. He didn't know how she did it.

"Does she think she's too good for you? Nobody's too good for you."

"I don't know, Ma. Don't worry about her. I hardly know her."

His mother played with his bedspread. "You like her. I can tell. You haven't been happy. Until now, but you will be. You deserve to be."

"I'm happy, Ma . . . honest."

"I want you to be happy," she said in a soft voice.

He turned to her. "You know what would make me happy," he said. He loved his mother, and he didn't want her to think that he was using her; but sometimes she made him feel like he had to beg. He didn't like that. He wanted to be the one who bought her presents, not the other way around. But right now, he needed something. He needed new clothes. New clothes always made him feel better.

When he left the house, he had ten dollars in his pocket, ten dollars that his mother had given him, and a kiss on the cheek, telling him to go get himself something nice.

He took the steps outside his house two at a time, almost running into Mrs. Fruchter, their upstairs neighbor.

"Sorry, ma'am," he mumbled quickly.

She smiled at him, almost beaming. "Why are you so happy? Good news?"

He grinned to himself and just nodded his head. People were so easily fooled. Good news. What good news? He was going to track down a girl whose parents thought he was no good for her. A girl who got him so confused he could barely talk to her without getting angry.

People really were fools. Or else, he had a special talent for fooling them. He walked across town to Beale Street. The ten-dollar bill was carefully folded into quarters, a tiny, neatly creased package, so small that it could fit into the deepest V of his pocket.

The closer he got to the Negro district, the taller he walked, fingering the folded bill in his pocket. He loped down the street, his stride long.

He liked walking in the streets filled with Negroes; he liked catching the beat of music coming from the bars; but mostly he liked that the men gave him side-long looks — nobody would challenge him, challenge his right to be there. It was a different walk than he had at work, or at home; and he loved it, felt older, felt good.

He stopped and crossed the street.

"Hey . . . man. . . . Hi . . . there." A small balding white man, his glasses glinting in the sun, greeted him like a long lost buddy.

"Beautiful day . . . beautiful day," chirped the man.

"Hello, Mr. Lansky." Elvis smiled a cool smile.

Mr. Lansky reached up and put his arm around Elvis' shoulders. "You look like you need something nice. Why don't you look inside? I've got a new shipment you wouldn't believe."

"That's why I came."

"I know, I know. Why don't you bring your friends?"

Elvis shrugged. What was he going to tell Mr. Lansky — that he didn't have any friends? At least not ones who wanted to shop on Beale Street. Bring anybody else with him? Never.

Not everyone had a mother like his who'd stake him to ten bucks, no questions asked. She was special. She never complained about his hair or the way he dressed.

Mr. Lansky grinned at him. "Go in, go in. . . . Look around. You'll see something you'll like, I promise you."

Elvis walked into the store, out of the sunshine. The tables were piled high with slacks and bright shirts.

Elvis went straight to the unadvertised specials. A well-dressed man was shopping the same table. Elvis looked at the pants the man was holding in his hand. Shiny black with a lime green inset along the seam.

"Where'd you find those?"

The man looked up at him. The bags under his eyes hung down like loose fleshpockets.

His nose looked as if he was an ex-prizefighter.

"You talking to me?"

"I like those pants."

"You do? A boy like you? These aren't boys' pants. They're men's pants."

"I like em. Where did you find them?"

The man laughed. "You don't back down."

"I don't want to fight. I just like those pants. You saw them first. If you want to buy them, I can't have them. But if you don't, I can."

"What about the fact I just tried them on. You'll be buying pants that a nigger wore."

"That don't bother me none."

"It don't?"

"No, sir." The "sir" slipped out.

The man barked a laugh. "Who you calling sir? I like that." He tossed the pants to him. "Go try them on, boy. I want to see this."

Elvis caught the pants one-handed. In the dressing room, he quickly got out of his jeans and put on the pants. They were pegged at the ankles and pleated at the waist. The waist band was a four-inch band that came to the bottom of his rib cage.

He turned to look at himself in the mirror, slouching just a little. He liked the way the pants felt on his legs — the loose material ballooning at his knees, the high waist band making his thin waist look even thinner.

When he turned, the lime-green color in the seam flashed in the mirror.

He smiled at himself. He practiced smiling

so that he didn't squinch up his eyes, trying to let the whites of his eyes show while he smiled as widely as he could. He had good healthy white teeth. He was proud of his teeth. They didn't look like a cracker's teeth.

He rubbed his hands over his hair, and then held them out in the air. His hands were full of grease. What could he rub them against? He couldn't get grease on the new pants. They weren't even paid for yet.

He heard a voice beyond the curtain.

"Boy, you coming out?"

"One minute," Elvis shouted. He picked up his old shirt and rubbed his hands on the inside. Then he pulled the curtain aside.

The man gave a low whistle.

"Do you like them?"

The man nodded. "Come out of there where I can see you."

He walked into the center of the store. The black man went to a counter and pulled out a skinny suede belt.

"Here," he said. "Put this on."

Elvis threaded the belt through the oversized loops and buckled it. The end hung down, over his crotch.

"No, no, boy. Didn't anyone ever teach you how to do your belt? Come here."

Obediently, Elvis shuffled over to him. The man whipped his belt buckle so it was riding over Elvis' left hip and then he snaked the end of the belt around and around the belt.

"There," said the man triumphantly. "Now you got the look."

Elvis walked over to the mirror. Oh lord, he liked the way he looked in those pants.

"You need a shirt," said the black man. He picked a loud Hawaiian shirt out of the pile. The shirt had pink hibiscus with green stems delicately tracing down the sides.

"This one's perfect," said Elvis. "How much it cost?"

"The shirts are two-fifty. The pants are five."

"I can take two shirts. Help me find another."

The man grinned at him. "I don't know what it is about you, boy. Do you always find someone to take care of you?"

He bristled. "My mama takes good care of me."

"I'm not saying anything against your mama, but you've sure got weird taste for a white boy."

"I just like these clothes, that's all."

The man laughed. "That's not all, boy, and you know that."

Elvis fingered the pleats of his pants. The man knew. He couldn't explain to any white kids why he *had* to have these clothes. These clothes would help him. Help him be the man he knew he was inside.

After he bought the clothes, Elvis walked to Easton's. He could see Amy again. Now he looked right.

But when he arrived at Easton's she wasn't there.

Easton smiled at him. "You look good," he said.

"Do you know where Amy Klinger is?" Elvis asked. "I thought she'd be here."

"She canceled this morning. Every Saturday Amy and her mother have a routine. They go shopping and to the Peabody for tea. But today Amy had a class picnic, so she left her mother on her own. Her mother was complaining. I don't have the faintest idea where the picnic is, though."

"Thank you, sir," said Elvis with a grin. The class picnic. He knew where to find her.

Easton stopped him. He put a hand on Elvis' new shirt. "You don't have to call me sir," he said softly.

Elvis shrugged his hand off. "Yes, sir," he said, and turned and left.

The class picnic. Last year, when it was Elvis' senior-class picnic, he had taken his guitar; and even though he thought he had a voice like a sick cow, his teacher had complimented him.

It wouldn't look out of place for an old alum to show up at the class picnic. It was always held at River Park. He'd just go home and get his guitar and then act as if he had just stopped by. It would be perfect.

Chapter 8

It was a warm, humid day. Carol and Amy were on opposite teams in the baseball game.

Amy walked to home plate, picked up the lightest bat. She was not a bad athlete. She could run fast, if only she could see the ball coming toward her. She struck out so often, it was embarrassing. Amy brushed off her madras plaid bermuda shorts.

"Get a hit, Skinny!" yelled Steve.

Amy looked out at the outfield. Carol was playing shallow center field. Carol was a lousy outfielder. If she could just pop one in Carol's direction, the chances were good that she would drop it.

"Not at me!" Carol shouted. "I see what you're planning."

Everyone on the field, including Amy, laughed.

"Don't worry, I haven't hit one yet."

Amy took a few practice swings.

She stepped up to the plate. It was worth trying her hardest. Her team was behind by one run. There were two outs, and this was the last inning. Joey was on base. The chances of Amy hitting a home run were about one in a thousand. She told herself just to try to get a hit so she could keep the game alive.

Then she saw Elvis, standing alone down the first-base line. He was dressed outrageously for a picnic. His pants were so full at the knees that they ballooned out in the wind, making him look like a clown.

He was wearing another loud shirt with huge pink flowers on it. He wore the collar turned up. His hands were in the deep pockets of his pants, and nobody was talking to him. He grinned at her.

Amy didn't know how or why he had shown up, but she was more determined than ever to get a hit.

The first pitch sailed in high, but she swung at it anyhow, almost throwing her shoulder out as she reached for the pitch.

"Wait for it, Amy. Don't be anxious." She heard Elvis' voice coming from the first-base line.

She squinted in his direction, and waved her bat at him.

"Ignore that creep," whispered Steve, behind her.

Amy didn't answer him, but she felt lighter, happier, glad to be in the batter's box.

She saw the next ball coming in as if it were as large as a beach ball. She heard the thud as the ball hit the bat, her wrists turning over.

The ball went up in the air. In any other game, it would be a pop-up; but with Carol in the outfield, the chance for an error was great.

Amy tore down the first-base line without looking up. But she saw Elvis clapping for her out of the corner of her eye.

"Take second, take second!" he shouted.

Amy didn't hesitate. She kept her head down and rounded first. Only halfway to second, did she look around and see that Carol had indeed missed her pop-up. The ball had rolled behind her, and the center fielder, Tony, a guy with a good arm, had picked it up.

"Slide, slide!" Elvis yelled.

Amy let her feet slip out and fell backward. Her heel caught on the dirt, and she ended up sprawled out flat, but her feet were touching the base.

She got up, brushed herself off, and grinned at Elvis.

Joey had scored on her hit, and now the game was tied. Jimmy Crane was the next batter. He hit a little blooping single, and Amy tore around third to score.

Her teammates surrounded her, clapping her on the back so hard that she staggered.

"I scored! I scored. We won!" Amy shouted, dusting off the dirt.

Joey congratulated her. "I'd call it more a comedy of errors."

"Who cares? We won."

She turned to find Elvis to thank him for

his coaching. He seemed to have disappeared. Suddenly she stopped laughing. "Where is he?" she asked.

"What was the creep doing here anyhow?" asked Joey.

"Where is he, Joey?" Amy insisted. "He's not a creep."

"Are you kidding? He got kicked off the football team because he wouldn't cut his precious hair. Now that's a creep. And he got about a D-minus average."

"He got a C average! The same as yours."

"How do you know that?"

"I know," exclaimed Amy. "Besides, he helped me out, didn't he? I wouldn't have scored that winning run without him coaching me."

"Yeah, but he doesn't belong here."

"Go suck eggs, will ya?" snapped Amy.

"Hey, is that any way for a winner to talk?" asked Carol, coming off the field. "Oh well, at least the game is over. Let's eat. I'm starved."

"Me, too, but I want to find Elvis. He just disappeared while I was on base."

Carol spotted Elvis, way down by the river, his back against one of the cottonwood trees. "There he is, but I still say he's creepy."

"Nobody asked you," snapped Amy. She ran toward the river and climbed down the embankment.

Elvis barely looked up. He had a guitar in his hand and he was humming in a low, low voice.

"Thanks for helping me to get the run. I looked for you afterward, but you disappeared. Why didn't you stick around and help me celebrate?"

He laughed, a hesitant, sarcastic laugh. "Yeah, sure."

"I mean it. You cheered for me to run. I would never have tried for second if you hadn't told me to."

"So I got you to second base. Big deal."

"Well, it was a big deal to me. I scored the winning run. I'm proud of that."

"It doesn't take much to make you proud, does it."

Amy stared at him. "That's mean. You know that? Thanks a lot. Do you always talk to girls like that? No wonder you don't have a real girl friend."

"Yeah, no wonder." He kept his head down and started playing again. It was a sad song, plaintive, and his voice was so low that she couldn't make out the words.

"I'm sorry," he mumbled.

"Sorry isn't enough," said Amy. "Why do you say such mean things? I didn't do anything to hurt you."

"I said I was sorry. Didn't you hear me?" He continued to strum his guitar. She wished she could see his eyes when he played, but he was facing the water, and short of wading into the river, it was impossible to look him in the face.

"Do you want me to go away?" she finally asked.

"It's a free country."

"That's my line."

Finally he put the guitar down and turned to her. His eyes looked friendly, not cold. He was teasing her.

"I didn't know you played guitar. You're good."

"I stink."

"That's not true."

He shrugged.

Amy picked at a blade of grass, and looked up the embankment to see if anyone was watching them. He followed her eyes. "Looking for your friends?"

Amy shook her head.

"Good, 'cause I don't feel too much like being beat up again."

"I wouldn't let them."

"Oh, yeah, my little protector."

"Why are you here if you're in such a bad mood?"

"Plenty of guys in my class came back for the picnic."

"I know, but . . . I thought maybe you came to see me again." Amy's voice was low.

Finally, he put down the guitar and turned to face her. "I did come to see you. I think about you all the time; but when I see you, I give you a hard time. I can't think of any reason for us to be together."

"How about that we like each other?"

"Yeah, you know what I found out? That you are number one in the class."

"That's not such a big thing. Everyone

thinks that good grades just come naturally to me, but they don't. I work for them. Getting to college is the only way that I'll get away from home. I need a full scholarship. I work for it."

He stared at her. Then he laughed. "I can believe it. Nothing comes for nothing. Not if you care about it."

"What do you care about? Music?"

"Naw . . . I stink at that."

"Then what do you care about?"

He shrugged. "I don't know. I care about how I look. That's important to me. I work at that."

"But . . . that's. . . ." Amy didn't know what to say. It seemed sad to her to care so much about the way you looked, especially if the way you looked was so strange. It just shouldn't be so important.

"It's important," said Elvis. "People see me and they know."

"Know what?"

"That I'm special."

Again Amy felt sad. Her friends didn't think he was special, they thought he was crazy. She couldn't think of anything to say. She leaned over and took his face in her hands. She kissed him on the lips.

At first his lips were closed tight. She tried to open them with her tongue, but he kept them closed.

Then he opened his lips and his tongue was in her mouth, filling it. He put his arms around her back and pulled her tight.

Chapter 9

Amy was the first to pull away from their kiss. Suddenly she was frightened. She had been the one to kiss him, just as she had been the one to invite him to her party. Girls were not supposed to be so forward. "Please don't think I'm cheap," she pleaded. "I don't act like this. I'm not cheap. This isn't me."

Elvis laughed. "This isn't me, either. Don't worry." He had a sarcastic edge to his voice that Amy didn't like.

"What do you mean?" she asked.

"I don't know. Kids think I'm just a dumb cracker who dresses weird."

"They don't think that."

He laughed again. "They do. Amy, stop foolin' around."

"Who's fooling around? That kiss wasn't fooling around!"

Elvis looked around, embarrassed. "You're talking too loud."

"Then tell me why I can't be your girl."

"We have nothing in common."

"Love doesn't always come to people who have a lot in common. Haven't you ever heard that opposites attract? It's a well-known chemical reaction. Trust me. I've studied chemistry."

Elvis laughed so hard that Amy was afraid that he might fall into the water. She got up quickly, turning red. How could she have mentioned the word *love* to him? Of course, he would hoot at her.

But he grabbed her. "Don't run away."

"You were laughing at me."

"I'm sorry. It's just when you start talking about love."

"Well, something happened to me the day I saw you. Why can't it be love? I'm certainly old enough. My mother was married when she was my age." Amy hesitated. She wasn't sure that her mother was a good advertisement for early marriage.

"I'm sorry I laughed," said Elvis.

"But you don't love me."

He shrugged. "Don't talk to me about love. Anybody who loved me would have a hard time."

"Why?"

"Because I'd demand total loyalty!"

The fierceness in his voice made Amy swallow hard. She wanted to prove herself.

"I'm a very loyal person," she said. "You just see me with my friends, and you think I'm just like everybody else. But I'm not."

"You're not, huh?"

"No. What do you think of me anyhow?

You kissed me as if you meant it, but then you won't talk about love. I don't understand you."

"Nobody does."

"Well, if I'm going to prove my loyalty, what do you want me to do?"

He smiled at her. "You're serious?"

"Well, it depends what you ask."

He giggled. "You're going to be my slave."

"I didn't say I'd be your slave."

"What's wrong?" he asked.

"Nothing," said Amy, almost too quickly.

"You looked as if I had said the secret word and a duck was going to land on your head." He smiled again, teasing her, as if trying to let her know that whatever secret he had read in her eyes would be safe.

Amy stood up. "All right, what's my first command?"

"Lunch."

"Lunch?"

"Yup . . . three hot dogs and a mess of potato salad. Can you carry all that?"

"You want me to bring it all to you?"

He looked out at the river. "I knew this wasn't going to work out."

"Well, boys usually get girls the food. It will look a little strange if I bring it to you."

"I thought you didn't care what people thought. You were the one who was supposed to be different inside."

"You're right. I was being stupid. Sorry."

"You'd better hurry, or I'll punish you."

Amy studied his face to make sure that he

was just kidding. He smiled at her, again that smile that separated the left side of his face, not quite a sneer, but not quite what you would expect, either.

He stood up and took her hand. "Forget it. I'll go get my own food."

"No, no," she said quickly. "You stay here, sire. I'll bring your food."

"Sire." He rolled the word around on his tongue, as if enjoying its sound. He waved his hand imperiously. "Go."

She scampered up the embankment.

The line for food was long. Carol was at the head of her line. She waved to Amy.

"Hey, end of the line," said the person standing behind Carol.

"I was saving this place for her," said Carol haughtily, giving the guy one of her best, most snobbish looks.

"Thanks," whispered Amy.

"What have you been doing, tell me?"

"Nothing," whispered Amy. "I was just talking to him."

"Talking, huh. . . . That's not what Joey says."

"Joey, what does he know about it?"

"He says he saw you necking down by the river. How could you do it in public with him? I told Joey that you had a bet with me. I tried to save your reputation. I said I bet you wouldn't kiss him, and you were just kissing him to win a bet. But come on, Amy. Everyone is talking about you. You can't possibly see anything in him. He's a nothing."

"He's not," whispered Amy. "Besides, Joey shouldn't have been spying on me."

"Joey likes you. If you'd give him a chance, you two could have a real thing going."

Amy thought about Joey — his ears that stuck out, his straight blond hair, and his thin lips. No, Joey was not at all what she wanted.

She knew what she wanted.

"Five hot dogs, please," Amy said.

Miss Sugarman gave her a shocked look. "Five!"

Amy held out two plates. "They're not all for me."

"I should hope not. It's two to a customer." Miss Sugarman put two hotdogs on each plate. "Besides, whoever you're getting it for could have come up herself."

"Or himself," muttered Carol behind her.

"Can I have an extra portion of potato salad?" Amy asked. "Please, ma'am? I'm very hungry."

Miss Sugarman took an ice-cream scoop full of potato salad and put one neat scoop on each of the plates that Amy was holding. "If you want seconds, you or your friend can come back after we've served everybody firsts."

"But, but . . . I'm extra-special hungry." Amy used her most wheedling voice.

Miss Sugarman was not amused. "Amy, it's not like you to be selfish."

Carol giggled. "It's not like Amy not to be perfect, you mean."

Miss Sugarman looked confused. "Go

along, Amy. You have plenty on your plate for two healthy appetites. Give the others a turn."

The relishes were placed on a separate picnic table. Amy took her plates over. She stared down at the hot dogs. He hadn't told her what he wanted on them. Mustard? Relish? The works?

She felt starved herself, but she took one of the hot dogs from her plate and put it on his. Then she took her scoop of potato salad and put it on the second plate, too.

"Going on a diet?" Carol asked.

Amy shook her head. "Stop giving me a hard time."

"Me, after I covered for you with Joey? Are you really going to give him all that food?"

"He asked for three hot dogs, he's gonna get three hot dogs."

"What else has he asked for that you've given him?"

"Look, I don't give you a hard time about what you and Steve do. Why can't you leave me alone about this?"

"If you're not careful, everyone is going to leave you alone."

Amy picked up two Cokes and tried to balance them on her plates. One of the Cokes tottered dangerously and began to fall. Carol caught it.

"Come on," she said. "Give me one of them. I'll help you."

Amy looked at her with relief. "Thanks. He's waiting for me down by the river."

"Yeah, sure . . . the frog prince. This I got to see."

"Well, the truth is he kisses real good."

Carol laughed. "How would you know? Who have you ever kissed outside of kissing games?"

"No one, but it wasn't disgusting."

"Amy, you're impossible. All your brains got stuck in your books or something."

"Why am I impossible?"

"Who else would think kisses might be disgusting? I just wish you'd fall for someone a little more your type."

"Maybe he is my type."

"Okay, okay, let's not argue that one again. If I don't get back to Steve soon, he'll think I've been kidnapped."

As they reached the bank of the river, Amy heard a deep voice singing. As she looked down at the riverbank, she was shocked to see a classmate, Diane Merckins, sitting on the grass very close to Elvis, listening to him sing as if she were looking up at Frank Sinatra.

"Looks like he already has company," said Carol. "I don't think he needs your hot dogs."

"What's she doing there?"

"She's more his style," said Carol. Diane was known as fast. She went to the USO dances where the Army reservists showed up, and everybody said that she made out with the soldiers, because she had already been through the senior class.

Elvis finished his song and spotted Amy and Carol up on the bank. He waved.

"Can't he even walk up the bank for his food?"

"Carol, please. You offered to help. Don't quit on me now."

Together they slipped down the muddy bank, trying hard not to spill the Cokes.

Elvis didn't get up. Instead, he picked up his guitar and started to sing another song.

Amy and Carol stood there, holding the plates of hot dogs, while Diane sang along during the chorus. Amy wanted to heave her hot dogs at him. She barely heard his voice as he sang.

Carol put her plate down and twirled her finger around her ear, the universal sign that she thought that Amy was crazy.

Amy stood there, not knowing what to do. Carol shrugged and headed back up the bank, but Amy didn't follow her. Instead, she waited like a slave for her master to acknowledge that she was there.

Chapter 10

Slave. To Amy the word was loaded. It was as if Elvis had tapped into her soul and read her most intimate fantasy, one that she had never told anyone. She had a daydream, one in which she was a slave in Roman times. Her master controlled her every move.

No one in the entire world knew about it. But had Elvis somehow guessed? Is that why he had given her such a sly look when he asked her to be his slave?

If not, why was she standing there with his plate of three hot dogs, while she had only one on her plate, and he sang to another girl?

Elvis finished singing. He smiled at Diane and then looked up at Amy. "Those for me?" he asked.

Amy nodded.

"Thanks."

Diane gave Amy a resentful stare. The edges of Diane's breasts showed along her halter line. Diane Mercken's big breasts were the only thing she had going for her. Amy wondered if Elvis went for big-breasted women.

"How did you get three hot dogs?" asked Diane. "I thought it was two to a customer."

"I've got clout," said Amy.

Elvis grinned at her. "That's my girl." He wolfed down the first hot dog in practically one bite, his cheeks puffed out with food.

Amy took a polite nibble on her hot dog, trying to look like Scarlett O'Hara in *Gone with the Wind*. Southern girls were not supposed to have big appetites.

"I think Elvis has a wonderful voice, don't you?" cooed Diane.

Elvis picked up the second hot dog. He shoved it into his mouth.

"Maybe, but his table manners aren't too good."

Elvis laughed with his mouth full. "No table," he said.

"Didn't your mama teach you not to talk with your mouth full?" Amy was laughing, too. She enjoyed the feeling that they were sharing a joke that left out Diane.

Elvis covered his mouth with his hand. "I guess when my mama's not here, my best girl teaches me."

Amy listened to the words *best girl*. Did he mean her?

"I'm pretty hungry myself," said Diane in a little-girl voice.

Elvis made no move to offer her any of his food.

"You'd better get up there quick," said

Amy sweetly. "Miss Sugarman was worried that they were running out."

Diane gave Elvis a last look and finally left in a huff.

Elvis finished eating and washed his hands in the river. He turned to Amy. "Let's go somewhere where we can be alone."

"I've got to help clean up," said Amy.

"That can wait." His hand was tight on hers, almost hurting, the way in her slave fantasy her owner held her.

"It can't wait. I promised." Amy was on the cleanup committee.

"What about tonight?" insisted Elvis.

Amy looked across the picnic grounds to where Carol and Steve and the others were picking up the litter from the picnic.

"Come help us clean up."

Elvis shook his head.

"Why not?"

"I don't feel like it. Okay?"

"Don't get so huffy. Why can't you just do normal things that would make things easier for you? It's not such a big deal to help clean up."

"I *don't* want to. What I want is to know if you're going to do my bidding. You're my slave. I've got something to do tonight, and I want to do it with you."

"I can't. I'm supposed to go to Carol's after the picnic." She paused. His eyes seemed to have turned from light blue to blue-black.

"How do you do that?" she demanded.

"What?"

"Change the color of your eyes?"

"I don't."

"You do. You get angry and your eyes change. It's scary."

He smiled at her, making his face go soft again. "I don't want to scare you. But why did you kiss me like that if you're not willing to go out with me? I thought you didn't care what your parents thought. Or are you a tease?"

"I'm not."

"I didn't think so."

"I've never kissed anybody like I did with you this afternoon," said Amy. "It just happened . . . but. . . ."

"Don't think about it. Just come with me tonight."

"But my father. . . ."

He let go of her hand. "You're right. Forget the kiss. Go back to your friends."

"Wait for me," Amy begged. "I'll get Carol to lie for me."

"I don't want you to get in trouble because of me." He had a sly look on his face that made her not believe him.

"Will you wait for me?" she asked impatiently.

He nodded.

She hurried across the grass. Carol glanced over at her. "What's the matter? Can't Prince Charming pick up a lousy piece of paper?"

"He isn't on our cleanup committee." Amy knew she sounded defensive.

"That's because he doesn't know the word

clean," joked Steve. "Do you think he ever washes his hair? That's how it stays so greasy."

"Don't start," warned Carol. "Amy's decided that he's a prince in frog's clothing, or a frog in prince's clothing. One or the other."

"I'd vote for the frog. He's got sort of frog eyes," said Steve.

Furiously Amy picked up a paper plate full of relish and threatened to heave it at Steve.

"Hey!" he shouted. "What did I do to deserve this?"

"Nothing, but you don't have to be so snide. I've helped you and Carol out when you needed it. Now I need help."

Steve looked uncomfortable. He kept glancing across the field at Elvis, leaning against a picnic table, his long legs crossed.

"I just need you to do for me what I've been doing for you. I'll be with him a few hours tonight. If my parents call, cover for me. I've done that for you, lots."

Carol and Steve looked at each other.

"What's the problem?" Amy demanded to know. "It's okay if I have to throw parties just so you can slow dance, but you won't do it for me. That's some friendship we've had for four years. For the first time, I want to do something more than just hang around with the two of you, and what do I get? That he's a greaser. Well, thanks a lot, I could have gotten that from my parents. You're supposed to be on my side."

"Amy . . . what if being on your side means

that you shouldn't be with him," asked Carol earnestly. "I'm not kidding. I think he's trouble. And he's dumb."

"Spare me. Don't you think that there might be something more important to a person than just grades? There is more to life."

Carol sighed. "That comes as quite a surprise from the class grind."

"Well, there's more to me, too. I thought you knew that."

"I just don't want you to get hurt."

"Everyone's always protecting me. I don't need it." Amy wondered. She was throwing herself at Elvis, like the cheapest slut in a bad movie. On the other hand, was she supposed to go to college so lily-white pure that she would never know what it was like to be French-kissed — to feel passion? Wouldn't it be more of a sin if she "practiced" with Joey, just because he was safe? The one thing she could say for sure about Elvis was that he was not safe.

Carol sighed. "Okay, Amy. You win. You seem so serious. I just wish he'd come talk to us."

"How can he when the last time he tried, Steve and Joey beat him up?"

"He didn't even fight back," Steve mumbled.

Carol stepped in quickly. "Let's not rehash that. Okay. I'll cover for you. I'll tell my mom that I'm meeting you at the Suzore Movie Theater. There's a double feature there. That way, Steve and I can meet there, and you can go there, too . . . with him. We can double-date."

Steve looked doubtful, as if what Carol was suggesting was slightly obscene.

Carol put her arm around Amy's waist. Her flesh felt warm, encircling, protecting. She walked Amy a little away from Steve. "Have fun," she whispered.

"Thanks." Amy's anger melted.

Carol laughed at her. "You're really something, you know that?"

Amy shook her head. "I don't know what I am. You seem to think I'm crazy."

"Yeah, well, a little, I do. But I've never seen you so serious about anything. Don't pay any attention to what Steve and Joey think. If you think he's right for you, you're the only one who knows your heart." Carol gave her an embarrassed smile, as if she knew that she was sounding pretentious, but Amy was grateful to her.

"Go on," said Carol, giving her a push. "Your frog prince is waiting for you."

Amy laughed. "Too late . . . I've kissed him already. If he was going to turn into a prince it would have happened already."

"Maybe it takes more than one kiss," suggested Carol.

Chapter 11

Amy stood with Elvis in front of Ellis Auditorium, staring up at the sign "All-Night Sing."

"I can't stay all night, El, I can't." Amy heard the whining tone in her voice, but she was scared. She had gone home and changed and lied to her parents, telling them that she would be spending the night at Carol's. Elvis had refused to tell her where they were going.

"It'll be a surprise," he said.

"But what should I wear?" she had asked.

"Something nice."

Amy chose a black sheath dress made of a rayon with a fine sheen to it. When Amy bought it, her mother had said, "This dress will take you anywhere." Amy imagined a little motor in the back of the dress.

"You look classy," Elvis had said approvingly when he picked her up at Carol's. But he still would not tell her where they were going. She had just never expected that they would go to a gospel sing.

Amy had heard it advertised on the radio — the Blackwoods, and Hovie Lister, and the Statesmen — but she had never gone to the gospel sings. Her parents would have been appalled.

"All night!" she repeated.

"It's not really all night. It's just a long show. All great music." He grinned at her. "It's going to be my treat."

"But . . . but . . . I can't — "

"Don't want to hear about it. This is something I've been wanting to take someone special to." He seemed to read the anxiety on her face. "It's not what you expected for our big date? It's better than the movies."

"Have you been to one of these before?"

"Uh . . . uh. . . . The All-Night Sings are the best." He emphasized the words *all night*. Amy had visions of explaining to her parents that she had spent the night with a boy they had forbidden her to see and what they had done was listen to gospel music!

They'd never believe her. Never! She looked around at the crowds rushing past her. She wished they could just be at the Suzore with Carol and Steve, having a more normal teenage date — a double feature and a little make-out in the dark.

Amy realized she was being unfair. There were plenty of teenagers going inside to the gospel sing, some she even recognized, but they weren't from her crowd. They nodded at

Amy, but no one said hello to Elvis. It was the same as at school; it was as if he were invisible.

She looked up at him. He seemed so excited, so sure that he was offering her a treat. Stop being such a snob, she told herself.

"Okay," she said, giving Elvis a grin. "In for a penny, in for a pound."

He gave her a quizzical stare. "What does that mean?" he asked belligerently.

"It's just something my parents say. It means I'm already in deep trouble just by being with you tonight. I can't get in much more trouble. In for a penny's worth . . . in for a pound's worth. A pound is money in England, sort of like our dollar."

He looked at her suspiciously as if she were making fun of him, talking too much like an intellectual. Amy was determined not to ruin this evening. She took his arm proudly, as if they were going to the Oscars. "Let's go," she said.

Inside, the stage was empty except for microphones and a gleaming grand piano dominating center stage. With Amy's hand secure in the crook of his elbow, Elvis gave his tickets to an usher as if he were taking his lady to the opera. The usher guided them down the center aisle.

With each step, Amy felt more and more conspicuous, but Elvis seemed to know exactly where his seats were. Finally the usher stopped only three rows from the stage. Amy had never sat that close to performers in her life.

"These must be the best seats in the house," she whispered.

Elvis preened. "I know one of the Blackwoods. You'll see. The Blackwoods go to our church, the First Assembly. Cecil and I are in the same Bible class. Afterward, I'll take you backstage."

How would he introduce her? Amy wondered. Would he call her "my girl"?

Just then she heard a drum roll, and five men came out — the Blackwoods. They wore bright red suits that glittered in the stage lights. Their hair made Elvis' hair look conservative. Each of the Blackwoods had four-inch-high pomadours that swept back from their temples in cascading waves.

A heavyset man sat down on the piano stool and began pounding out a fast rhythm. The rhythm was so strong that Amy found herself clapping with the beat. Her feet wouldn't stay still. She pounded the floor with the rest of the audience, thousands of feet making the auditorium shake. Each time she thought the song was over, the quartet teased the audience with another high-pitched falsetto.

She felt lifted right out of her shoes, out of her dress, out of her books, out of her soul. Finally the music stopped, and as the applause died down, she glanced over at Elvis. He wasn't shouting and stomping like the others. It was as if he was studying. He had a look of such serious concentration on his face that she felt it would be an intrusion to touch him. He looked untouchable.

She turned her attention back to the stage. The applause had died down, and the man at the piano was talking of love. He seemed to be looking directly at Amy. He talked about the love between man and woman, boy and girl . . . and the highest love, the love of sacrifice . . . for God sacrificed His only son for us. He spoke of love and joy and happiness.

Amy kept her eyes fastened on him. Love. Love and sacrifice she knew about. But joy? *Joy* was not a word used in her home. Would all her good grades bring her joy? She felt full of joy and love. It was impossible to listen to that music and want to sit still.

She glanced back at Elvis. He caught her eye, and he no longer had that studied, closed look. "You liked it, didn't you?" he whispered.

Amy nodded, but *liked* seemed such a mild word for what she felt.

The time went so fast that the performance was over before Amy realized it. She had expected to be bored the way she was at the opera that her mother made her listen to on Sunday afternoons, but this music hadn't bored her. Far from it.

At the end of the performance, Amy stood up to leave with the rest of the crowd, but

Elvis put his hand on her forearm. "Wait," he commanded. "We're going backstage in a minute."

"You're kidding."

He shook his head. "I told you before. I know the Blackwoods. How come you didn't believe me?"

Amy still wasn't sure whether she believed him or not. It sounded too much like the kind of a story someone might make up to impress a date.

Elvis stood up, his hands automatically smoothing his own long hair and sideburns.

Amy patted her hair. She could feel the hair spray. "Do I look all right?" she asked.

Elvis gave her a slow look, up and down, and smiled. "Pretty . . . pretty as can be."

She shook her head. "You know, you make me feel pretty."

He laughed. "Come on, you know you're pretty. You bounce down the streets like you own them."

Could he really be talking about her? Did she look pretty when she walked down the street? Didn't he see that her nose was too big, that her legs were too skinny?

He laughed again. He bent down and kissed her on the nose. "Come on, I'm gonna show you off!"

They walked toward the front of the stage, past the salmon-colored gladiola displays. A long line of people snaked back from the stage door, holding out their programs, hoping for an autograph. A fat man dressed in a shiny blue suit was standing guard over the stage door.

"Can I take my girl backstage?"

The fat man nodded. The line in front of Amy parted for them. She felt a sense of power, a feeling that she belonged to the inner circle.

They walked through a small steel door to the side. Elvis kept a protective hand on her elbow.

The backstage area was cramped and cruddy. The cement walls were streaked with mildew, and the big communal dressing room wasn't much more luxurious than the girls' locker room at Humes.

Elvis nodded to the men and women backstage.

"How do you know them all?" Amy whispered.

"I come to almost every show," he said softly, his voice not quite a whisper.

"But how did you meet them all?"

He shrugged. "I told you. One of the Blackwoods' brothers goes to Sunday school with me."

Elvis was so strange. He didn't seem to have any friends, but then it turned out that he could get backstage when he wanted; and these professionals greeted him a little bit like a mascot, but with a certain amount of respect.

"Amy, I want you to meet James Blackwood."

Amy turned. It was the first time in her life that she had ever met a performer in person. She could feel her head bobbing up and down.

"I loved your show," she gushed. "You were wonderful." She knew she sounded goopy.

"What's your name again, sweetie? Old El said it so softly that he must want to keep you to himself."

"Amy." It required extraordinary mental concentration to remember her name. Never had she felt like such an idiot, but Mr. Blackwood seemed to have enough charm not to notice that she was blabbering. In fact, he seemed to enjoy the fact that she was so flustered. He was in no hurry to end the conversation. Close up, she realized he was smaller than he looked onstage, quite a bit shorter than Elvis; and his eyes had deep circles underneath them.

"You know, you're the first girl Elvis has brought around here. And what a pretty one, too! We were beginning to wonder about old El. He'd just come back here, asking questions, pestering all the time. But no girls."

Amy glanced up and saw that Elvis' eyes had narrowed, but he was still grinning shyly.

Suddenly, she wanted to make her own mark. She wanted to say something that would make Mr. Blackwood remember her and while she was doing it she wanted him to stop teasing Elvis. She felt protective of him.

James Blackwood might be the performer, but his crude flirting with her made him just a show-off.

"Elvis has the pick of girls," she said. "Probably he doesn't bring them around 'cause he doesn't want to make you feel bad."

Elvis laughed loudly. James gave her a knowing grin, as if he understood what she was trying to pull off.

She smiled. She had never felt so grown-up and in control in her life.

Chapter 12

It had started raining when they got out of the auditorium. The crowds were gone, and the streets looked empty and a little forbidding.

Amy looked at her watch. It was five after eleven. Elvis held the door of the pickup open for her. She felt her tight skirt climb up the back of her thigh as she took the high step from the ground to the truck. She turned her head and caught Elvis staring at the curve of her leg. She wondered if the seam of her stocking was crooked.

"Enjoying the view?" she asked as she slowly brought her leg inside the pickup, turning on the seat, so that now she was facing Elvis, and she brought her ankles trimly together.

"Uh . . . huh." He leaned over and kissed her quickly on the lips. Then he closed the door and walked around the front of the pickup. The sense of being that high up off the street gave her a feeling of being protected and powerful.

"I like driving in a truck."

He smiled at her. "Why?"

She shrugged. "I don't know." Then she giggled. "It makes me feel like a man."

He laughed loudly. "You're one funny girl, you know that? You're smart and you're funny and I like your spirit. And you're sexy."

Amy glowed. Most boys liked that she was funny, and a good sport, but Elvis was the first boy to find her both sexy and funny. She moved closer to him on the seat. He put his arm around her. The streets were almost deserted.

They passed the turnoff for Carol's house. "Where are we going? I've got to get back to Carol's by twelve. That's her curfew on weekends and if I'm later Carol's mother might call my mother. I'm supposed to be spending the night with Carol, remember."

Elvis pointed up to the sky. "Forget about Carol. See that moon. We're heading for it."

"El . . . it's nearly eleven. I've got to get back."

"Got to . . . got to — "

"I know. It's boring. But — "

"Look . . . we'll just go get a little air. Just a little drive out by the river. It's such a sweet night. Please. You were so terrific back there. I love having you be my girl." He pressed her shoulder as if to remind her that he was indeed real.

"I promise, you won't get in trouble. I won't get you in trouble."

She wanted to tell him that his promises didn't count. He couldn't promise that. But why did she always have to play it so safe? She didn't. Teenagers were supposed to have a little rebellion in them. Why not her?

As they drove along the curves of the road, Amy's body was pulled closer to Elvis. The moonlight bent the tree shadows into beautiful patterns. She could catch glimpses of the moonlight on the Mississippi. She leaned her head against Elvis' chest.

"You want to really feel like powerful?" he asked.

Amy's back stiffened. His voice had a mocking tone in it that made her feel that she had gone too far, and that he was trying to remind her that he was in control.

"Take the wheel," he said.

"What?"

"Well, you can't get the feel of a pickup without driving one."

He took his hands off the wheel, spreading them wide.

"What are you doing?" asked Amy. But she laughed. This was how her father had taught her to drive. The truck slowly began to veer toward the right shoulder of the road.

Elvis just laughed. His foot was still on the gas pedal.

Amy took the wheel, moving over so that the upper part of her body was pressed against him. She could feel the muscles of his right leg tense as the road curved, but he didn't take the wheel from her, and he didn't take his foot off the gas pedal.

She kept her hands on the wheel, beginning to enjoy the sense of control that holding the wheel gave her.

"Move over here," said Elvis, scrunching himself against the window of the truck. "You'd better take the gas pedal, too."

As he took his foot off the accelerator, the car began to slow down and became more difficult to steer. Amy looked ahead.

They were climbing the hill by the bank of the river. The road was turning. She needed some gas if she was going to make the turn. She reached her foot down for the gas pedal, but she pushed Elvis' foot by mistake. The truck surged ahead. "The accelerator's stuck!" he said.

An oncoming car was nearly on top of them. She could feel the wind from the passing car through the open window. They missed each other by inches. She could see the driver cursing at them.

She managed to negotiate another turn, but the truck was like a monster that had come alive.

"I'll try to get the accelerator unstuck," Elvis said. "You keep driving." He bent down in an awkward position, trying to fit his body underneath the steering wheel.

Once again Amy saw headlights coming toward them, around the bend.

"Oh God, it's another car," she whispered. "Be careful."

Amy concentrated with all her might, trying to keep the pickup on the road. She could feel Elvis on the floor of the pickup, trying to push the accelerator free. She tried to keep her feet out of his way.

The other car came closer.

"Be careful!" Amy whispered.

Her words were too late. She managed to avoid the car, but instead of getting the accelerator unstuck, Elvis had somehow pushed it all the way to the floor.

The truck jumped, as if it had been hit by lightning. Amy couldn't reach the brake to try to control the skid. The truck careened across the road and tore through the guard rail.

Amy heard Elvis screaming. Then she felt her leg bending. Something was pressing against it as the truck kept going forward.

Then finally there was a lurch as the gas pedal suddenly became unstuck and the truck's wheels began to churn in the soft mud of the riverbank.

But then Amy heard a crack. No pain, but it was the worst sound she had ever heard. The crack of bone was a thick, rich sound, very different from the snapping of a twig.

Chapter 13

Amy had torn her cheek on the lock button of the door, and for the moment her cheek hurt much more than her leg. Her breath came in gasps.

"Are you all right?" Elvis was leaning over her. The truck seemed to be balanced right on the edge of the river. She could hear the water.

"Are you okay?" she whispered.

"I think so. I got a knock on the head, but I didn't pass out. What happened?"

"We just missed a car coming at us and then the next thing I knew the truck jumped and we. . . ." She couldn't talk anymore. She started to sob.

"Easy, honey . . . easy. We've got to get out of the truck," he said. "I smell gas. It might explode."

"I can't. My leg — "

"What's wrong?"

"I think it's broken."

"SHIT!" He slammed his fist hard against

the dashboard. Amy felt as if she was going to throw up.

"I'm sorry."

"Amy. Don't say that. It's my fault. I wasn't mad at you. But look, I've got to move you."

"Elvis, no . . . I read in first aid . . . it's wrong to move someone if they might have broken something."

"It's wrong to die in a truck that might explode or dump in the river. I'll be careful. I'll come around to your side."

"Don't leave me!" She paused, knowing that she sounded hysterical. "I'm sorry. I know you've got to get me out the other side, but what if the pickup goes into the river when you get out?"

"I don't want to drag you out this side. Just relax. I'll be there in a second."

He left her alone. She stared out the dashboard, wondering when the pain would start. In the seconds that she was alone, she felt a peculiar floating sensation, as if she were no longer responsible for her survival. What would happen would happen.

She saw Elvis' face appear in the window. "The door's locked," he shouted.

Amy twisted to try to get to the lock, and that's when the pain hit, as if red-hot oil connected her leg to her brain.

"Oh God," she groaned, but she got the lock open. Then she must have passed out.

She woke up feeling wet. She was on a sandy shoal by the riverbank. She could see the ripples of the water just inches away. Her head was cradled in Elvis' lap. He was stroking her forehead.

He grinned slowly. "How are you feeling?"

"Not so good." She was frightened. Why wasn't she in a hospital? The pain in her leg was almost unbearable. Was she going to die out here? Even though the night was warm she felt as if she were freezing. Her teeth began to chatter.

"How long was I out?"

"Just seconds. I lay you down here, 'cause it's flat, but I've got to get up to the highway to get you help."

She squeezed her eyes together. She didn't want to be left alone by the river's edge. She felt a primitive fear that the river might grab her . . . even want her.

He stroked her forehead again. "I'm sorry," he whispered. "This is all my fault."

"It's not. . . . Accidents happen. It was my fault."

"Yeah, but you're the one who's hurt."

Amy wasn't sure that she liked how quickly he agreed that it was her fault. She wanted to be told that "fate" had caused the accident — that it was nobody's fault.

"Your teeth are chattering." He took off his jacket and wrapped it around her shoulders. "You're in shock. Don't faint on me again."

"I'm scared."

"No kidding. Lady sweet, you're the bravest girl I've ever known. You're hurt, and instead of having hysterics the way most girls would, you quietly say you're sorry. You keep your head. You have a right to be scared."

Amy found herself laughing and crying at the same moment. "I got to tell you a secret," she whispered.

He shook his head. "Can't it wait till I get help?"

Amy shook her head. She felt protected with her head in his lap. Though she was scared and hurting, there was something private about the river, the night, and the pain.

"What's your big secret? You can't say I got you pregnant, not after a kiss. Or did you think that's how babies were made?"

"Don't be disgusting."

"Sorry . . . I'm taking advantage of you. But you sounded so serious."

"I am. I'm about to tell you something I've never told anyone before."

"Listen, I know you're hurt. I know you're in shock. It's keeping the pain away, but I honestly don't think you're dying. Your leg *is* bent funny, and we need to get you some help. But I don't think you need to make any death-bed confessions."

"This isn't a death-bed confession, but it's something I want to say."

His arm went across her breast, cradling her. "Okay, sweetheart . . . I'm listening."

"I have this fantasy. . . . I tell it to myself before I go to sleep. I'm always a slave . . .

in Roman times. Remember that movie we had to see in school . . . with Marlon Brando as Mark Anthony?"

He nodded, wondering where this was leading. Her hand clutched his forearm, digging into it. She had a cut along her cheek, and her face looked pale, pale white in the moonlight.

"Is that your secret?" he asked softly.

She nodded, embarrassed to go on. But she felt she had to. "I'm always hurt. I get whipped and Mark Anthony saves me . . . in my daydream."

"Now you're really hurt," he said.

She nodded and started to cry. "It's better in my daydream," she sobbed. "Real pain hurts."

"I know," he whispered. He kissed her. His lips were soft. "You're going to be all right. I don't just mean tonight. I'm gonna take care of you. I promise."

Suddenly the pain came back, flooding her body. Now her fantasies seemed sick. Who could enjoy being in pain? It hurt too much.

She winced. Elvis gently lifted her head off his lap and stood up. "I've got to go up to the highway to get help. But wait here. I'll get something for you."

"I'm not likely to move anywhere," she said.

"Right."

Alone, she tried to keep the fear and pain away from her, as if they were visitors from outer space who could be made to disappear through an effort of will.

Seconds later, Elvis was back at her side. He had a capped Coke bottle in his hand.

"I don't want Coke."

"It's not Coke. Drink it." His voice had a note of command in it that made Amy obey. She took a gulp from the bottle.

She gagged. The liquid burned her throat. "What is this?"

"Moonshine, my daddy's. It's powerful. It'll help the pain."

"I feel like a wounded soldier in the Civil War."

"Yeah, and I'm Scarlett O'Hara." Elvis laughed. She took another swallow. This time it didn't burn quite as much.

Elvis made a splint out of dead branches and twine from the truck. Amy watched him. He had the same look of concentration that he had during the concert.

"How did you learn about first aid?"

"You had it, too . . . at Humes."

"Yeah, but I'm not sure I could really do it."

"You could."

He finished his splint. "I don't know how much good that'll do, but it'll help."

"I'm sure," she agreed, taking another sip. With each sip she felt warmer and more numb.

"I'm going up to the highway now. I won't be far. Will you be okay? I don't want to move you again until I can get somebody to help me."

He leaned over and kissed her on the lips. "Love you," he said softly.

"Me, too." Her words were slurred.

She closed her eyes for a second. The pain was awful, but somehow it almost felt as if it wasn't part of her. Her eyes snapped open. "Elvis!" she cried. "Are you there?"

"I'm right here, honey. Don't worry. Someone *has* to come along," he yelled to her.

She reached over and grabbed the bottle, surprised by how little there was left.

"Sing to me. Sing me a lullaby," she yelled, "so that I'll know you're still there."

She heard his low laugh. Then he began to sing, "Hush little baby, don't you cry...."

He sang slow and sweet. Amy took a last swallow from the bottle. Then she closed her eyes again.

She didn't know how much later she heard Elvis yell to someone, "She's down here!"

She felt herself being picked up in what seemed like dozens of arms and carried to a car.

She lay down along the backseat of a car and passed out again.

Chapter 14

Amy felt herself being lifted and placed on a metal dolly. Her leg felt tender and puffed, but still numb. She felt sorry for it, as if it were a good friend who had been hurt. She knew they had arrived at the hospital and she was relieved, as if the responsibility for surviving was no longer her own.

She saw Elvis standing in a corner of the emergency room. His hair was a mess; his shirt, torn. He looked pale, almost sickly white. His eyes darted around the hospital corridor. She called to him, and he came and took her hand, but he had a trapped look in his eyes.

People in green coats were running around, asking her questions. She gave her name and told them her phone number.

"Oh God, my parents," she said. "Please don't worry them."

"It's a little late for that," snapped the nurse. "You should have thought of that before you drank."

"I didn't drink. We weren't drinking."

"I just gave her a swallow for the pain," said Elvis. His voice was so low, Amy could barely hear it.

"Teenagers!" snapped the nurse. "You're all more trouble than you're worth."

Elvis flashed the nurse a filthy look. He gave Amy's hand a squeeze. "Don't worry. I won't leave you with her."

Then someone gave Amy a shot.

When she woke again, she was in a hospital room. Her leg was immobile, wrapped in a cast that started about six inches below her hip and extended to her toes.

She looked across the room and saw her mother asleep in a straight-backed chair. Her mother's head was pushed back at an unnatural angle.

Amy heard a wheeze from the other bed in the room. An old lady was having a coughing fit.

"Are you okay?" Amy whispered.

The old woman couldn't catch her breath to speak, but she waved a bony arm at Amy and smiled.

Amy's mother woke up with a start. "Amy. Oh my God!"

"Mom," whispered Amy. Her mother was across the room in a flash, as if she had been ejected from her chair. She grabbed Amy's hand.

"Oh my God . . . my God. Amy! Amy!"

Amy knew that she should be feeling

terrible and guilty. Why did she have an irrepressible desire to giggle?

"I'm okay, Ma."

"Okay!" Her mother's voice rose to a crescendo. "Okay! You dare to say you're okay . . . lying here in a hospital bed?"

"It doesn't hurt too much."

Amy's mother looked over at the other bed for sympathy. "Can you believe it? She's with some crazy guy . . . a nothing . . . a high school dropout."

"He graduated from high school, Ma."

The old lady in the bed started coughing again. Amy had the distinct feeling she was laughing.

"He looks like a high school dropout. Wait till your father gets ahold of him. Drunk driving!"

"Nobody was drunk!"

"That's not what the nurse said."

"She was a creep. She was awful."

"Amy," snapped her mother. "That's no way to talk about someone in the helping profession."

The lady in the next bed gave a loud cough. This time it distinctly sounded like a guffaw.

"Are you all right?" Amy's mother asked, although she sounded annoyed.

The lady waved a bony hand again. She shook her head.

Amy's mother returned her attention to Amy. "I can't believe you did something like this. Well, you see where you ended up. Oh my God, Amy, your father almost had a heart attack."

Amy put her head back on the pillow. She wished that it was a fantasy, and she had been hurt for a good cause. It seemed so unfair to have a broken leg *and* to be in trouble.

"Can I have some water?" she whispered. Her mother's expression changed, and Amy knew that giving her something to do was the right move. At least if she played on her mother's sympathy, she might gain some time.

Just then a nurse opened the door. It was the same nurse from the emergency room. Amy wondered if it was her imagination or if the nurse really did give her a dirty look. The nurse was followed by a man in his twenties in a white coat. He took quick, short steps as if he had too little time.

He went right to the bed of the old woman. He looked at her chart. Then he took the old lady's pulse and frowned. Amy wished that she was sharing the hospital room with someone a little younger and healthier. Even looking at the old lady gave her the creeps.

"Doctor, is she going to be okay?" Amy asked. "She was coughing a lot."

"You're next. I'll be with you when I'm done here." He didn't smile and he didn't answer Amy's question.

The doctor wrote something down on the old lady's chart and then moved over to Amy's bed. He examined her cast as if it were a piece of furniture that he admired.

"How are you feeling?"

"Okay. How bad is it?"

Again he didn't answer her question. Instead he addressed Amy's mother. "I'm afraid the alcohol level in her blood was high when they brought her in."

"Mama, I wasn't drinking."

The doctor looked at her skeptically. "The blood tests don't lie."

"No . . . I mean, I wasn't drinking before I got hurt. My date gave me something just to kill the pain. He wasn't drinking, either."

"He shouldn't have given you anything to drink," said the doctor sternly. "You could have gone into convulsions from the shock."

"He was trying to help me."

"Your leg *was* in a decent splint," admitted the doctor grudgingly.

Amy closed her eyes. Her leg, although perfectly still, felt as if it were vibrating, as if pain could come at any moment.

"How bad am I hurt?" she finally asked.

"It's a clean break, not too bad. You should be fine."

"What happened to Elvis? Was he hurt? The last thing I remember, he was holding my hand. He wouldn't leave me unless you made him."

"Him!" cried her mother. "Of course we made him leave when we got here. He was lucky your father didn't kill him. Why right now, your father is talking to Uncle Ben's lawyer. Somebody is going to pay."

"No!" shouted Amy. "It was my fault as

much as his. You'll sue him over my dead body!"

"Amy!" whispered her mother. "Hush." Her mother made a birdlike motion with her chin, warning Amy not to talk in front of the doctor.

Amy was furious. She could not, would not allow her parents to sue.

"He doesn't have any money. They're poorer than we are. You can't do that!" Amy was nearly screaming. The doctor looked embarrassed.

"He broke your leg," said her mother.

"He did not break my leg. An accident broke my leg. Accidents happen!"

"You don't know anything about a broken leg," hissed her mother.

"It's my leg," screamed Amy. "It's not yours."

The doctor put his hand on Mrs. Klinger's arm. "Look, you're both emotionally upset. Your daughter needs rest, and so do you."

"Crazy," muttered her mother. "Kids are crazy today. Doctor, she's a good girl. She's number one in her class, going to go to college, *if* they'll still have her after this!"

"Ma, I don't think Tennessee State Teachers College is going to withdraw a scholarship because I have a broken leg."

"You never know," sniffed her mother. "We trusted you."

Amy closed her eyes again.

The doctor coughed. "I think this is something you'll have time to go into later. We'd like to release Amy tomorrow. We'll just keep her overnight to see if the pain is a problem. It's really not a bad break."

Her mother gave the doctor a suspicious look, as if even he couldn't appreciate the tragedy of a broken leg.

"Please, Ma, he's right," said Amy. "Go home. You need rest. You've been up all night. I'll be okay."

"I don't want to leave you alone."

"Your daughter will probably sleep again," said the nurse. "You can't stay here all day."

Amy's mother leaned over the bed. Amy could smell the rose-scented talcum powder that was so familiar. Suddenly Amy felt like crying. Her mother kissed her on the cheek, looking in her eyes. Amy didn't know what to say to her. But finally she was gone, and all Amy felt was relief.

The old woman across the bed coughed again. Amy looked over at her. "Are you all right?" Amy asked.

"If you're going to ask me that every time I cough, we're going to have a very boring conversation," said the lady. "Don't give me that prune face, dearie. I didn't mean it as an insult."

Amy laughed. "Was I looking like a prune?"

"Definitely . . . either that or like you were sucking lemons."

"I'm sorry."

"Save the I'm sorrys for your mother. You'll need them. I'm Gloria Hunter."

Amy introduced herself. "I'll try not to ask you if you're all right too much."

"Don't worry about it. To tell the truth, you're better company than my last roommate."

"What was wrong with her?"

"She died."

Amy didn't like the idea that she was lying on the same bed where someone had just died. Nor did she think she wanted to talk to this old lady who might die at any moment. Amy was sorry now that she had told her mother to leave.

The woman laughed. "Don't ever play poker. Did anyone ever tell you that everything you feel shows on your face? I only sound like I'm dying. I've had that cough forever. I broke my hip. That's all that doctor cares about. So since you're only here for one night, you don't have to worry about me dying on you."

"I'm glad. I hope you last more than one night."

The women coughed again. "Thanks . . . that's probably more than my children hope for."

"Oh no," said Amy. "I'm sure they care."

"What makes you so sure?" asked the woman sharply.

"But if they're your children, they have to care."

The woman glanced at her. "I don't believe in have to. Anyhow, that's too depressing a subject. Let's talk about something cheerier.

Tell me about your boyfriend. He's cute. More than cute . . . downright handsome. He looked in on you while you were sleeping."

"He did?"

The woman nodded. "Your parents chased him away. He's a handsome guy."

"You thought he was handsome? Most people think he's ugly."

"I'm not most people." She had another coughing fit.

"No, I guess you're not."

The old woman grinned at her. "You're not so dumb yourself," she said.

"Thank you," said Amy politely. Amy lay her head down on the pillow and closed her eyes. She saw the accident happening again. Accidents were so strange. Minutes before the accident all she had been worried about was getting back to Carol's house before Carol's parents discovered she was with Elvis. Now everything was different. The accident had changed everything.

Chapter 15

Amy's armpits ached, but she had managed to swing up and down the corridor on her crutches. Betsy, a nice young nurse, was teaching her how to maneuver on crutches, even getting Amy to go up two wooden stairs that the hospital had for practice on crutches. Betsy taught Amy always to keep her weight behind her, going both up and down the stairs. It was like learning a complicated balancing act.

"Be careful," warned Betsy, as Amy got ready to try the stairs again.

"I have to get it right. My bedroom's on the second floor, and I'll die if I have to sleep in the living room."

Betsy looked down the corridor. "I think you have a visitor," she said.

Amy tried to turn her head. She had already learned she could make no sudden moves on crutches. It was as if she was having to learn to do everything in slow motion.

Elvis stood in the hospital corridor with a giant teddy bear in his hands. It had cute button eyes, and a pink tongue, but it looked like a toy a new father might bring for a baby girl.

"Look at me," Amy said with a smile. "I can move."

"Congratulations!" He gave her a lopsided smile. "Are you okay?"

She nodded, so pleased that he had managed to come during the few hours her mother wasn't at the hospital. "Come on," she said. "Watch me fly back to my room."

"No flying," warned Betsy. "Remember, that leg is just set."

"I'm just joking."

"She's quite a girl to be joking with a broken leg, isn't she?" asked Betsy.

Amy liked the way that Betsy praised her in front of Elvis.

"Can I do anything to help?" Elvis asked. He hovered over her as if he wanted to pick her up and carry her.

Amy shook her head. "No . . . it's easier if no one touches me. Then I lose my balance."

Elvis immediately looked guilty.

"Don't look like that. My mother is making enough of a tragedy out of this. You don't have to. It's not that bad. I'll be in a walking cast soon."

"It's still all my fault."

"It isn't," said Amy. "Don't say that. Particularly if my parents are around." She didn't want to tell Elvis that her father was thinking of suing him. Somehow she'd find a way of stopping her parents.

"Your parents really hate me."

Amy didn't answer. She placed her crutches in front of herself and swung her weight onto them, moving down the hall.

Elvis followed her, carrying the teddy bear. In her room, Mrs. Hunter, the old lady in the bed next to her, was awake. "Hi, Mrs. Hunter," said Amy.

"How did you do on your crutches?" asked Mrs. Hunter.

"Not bad."

Elvis put the teddy bear down on Amy's bed. It took up most of the bed.

"Where is Amy going to sleep?" asked Mrs. Hunter.

"I'll find room. Mrs. Hunter, this is my friend Elvis." Amy felt a flush of pleasure at being able to introduce Elvis to somebody away from her real life, someone who wouldn't and couldn't make a judgment whether he was "good enough" for her or not. She had come to like Mrs. Hunter, who treated her like a real person, not a child.

"How do you do, ma'am? We met briefly last night."

Mrs. Hunter beamed at him. "My, you're handsome," she said.

"Why thank you, ma'am," said Elvis politely.

Mrs. Hunter started to laugh and then her laugh turned into her horrible cough.

"Can I get you anything, ma'am?"

Mrs. Hunter shook her head. She took a sip of water.

"She doesn't like it when you pay too much attention to her cough," Amy whispered.

Mrs. Hunter lay back on her bed. "Don't you whisper in front of me. I always hated whispering."

"I'm sorry," said Amy.

"I told you the only thing I hate more than whispering is someone saying I'm sorry all the time."

Elvis laughed.

"Now, what's a handsome guy like you doing laughing?" asked Mrs. Hunter. "Don't you think this little girl here is special?"

Elvis nodded. "Yes, ma'am, I do."

"Well, I can see you have sense." She scrutinized Elvis as if he were a species of animal she enjoyed. "Come a little closer, boy," she said.

Elvis glanced over at Amy, who was resting on her bed, cradling the teddy bear in her arms. He stood by Mrs. Hunter's bed. He looked down at her. "Are you a gypsy?" he asked.

Mrs. Hunter shook her head. "Do you think if I were a gypsy I'd be alone here right now? Why, gypsies have so many kin they'd never let one of their own sit in the hospital alone. When a gypsy's sick, the other gypsies just camp out in the hallway."

"Don't you have children?" asked Elvis.

"I do. But they got better things to do than worry about me. But that's all right. I've been telling your friend Amy, as long as your brain is working, there's something to enjoy in life. Look at me. If I had died yesterday, I wouldn't have met you."

"I'm that special," mocked Elvis.

Mrs. Hunter looked serious. "You are. And so's Amy. I don't go telling that to just anybody."

"Well, you and my mama are about the only ones who think that," said Elvis.

The IV was hooked to Mrs. Hunter's left hand, but her right one was free. She looked over at Amy.

"Sweetheart, put that teddy bear down. He gave you that so that you'll have something to hug when he's not here. Right? But he's here. You can hug him now. You've got the real thing. Ain't that right?"

Elvis shrugged.

"Don't shrug your shoulders at me. Give that girl a kiss."

"You sure do like to order people around," said Amy.

"It's one of the greatest pleasures of old age. Don't knock it."

"We're not going to kiss in front of you," said Amy. "It wouldn't be right."

"Why not? I ask you. Just because it might give me a little pleasure?"

Elvis pushed his lips out. "It would really give you a kick to see us kiss?"

Mrs. Hunter nodded.

Elvis took the teddy out of Amy's arms and gave her a kiss on the lips right in front of Mrs. Hunter. He let her go and then sat on the edge of the bed, facing Mrs. Hunter. He grinned at her. "Did that satisfy you?"

Mrs. Hunter cackled. "It would take more than that to satisfy me. But it was nice. Sonny, it gives me pleasure to see a kiss like that. I know what you're thinking. That I'm a dirty old lady. Now come over here." She indicated the side of her bed with her free hand.

Elvis did what she asked. "You and Amy must get along," he said. "You both like to tell people what to do. And you both like to think you can read other people's minds."

"Now, you take that teasin' tone out of your voice," warned Mrs. Hunter. "I'll have you know that when I was in vaudeville, I did a mind-reading act that sometimes gave me the willies. Oh, it was staged, all right, me and the Great Zamboni. We had a code worked out, but sometimes someone in the audience would just jump out at me, and I knew ... *knew* what was wrong with them."

She lay her head back on the pillow. "It was the dying ones that reached out to you. ... I always knew. It scared me. I could read their minds like their skulls were books wrapped in glass for all to see."

Elvis took her hand and gently stroked it. She raised her head and smiled at him.

"Forgive me. I'm just an old lady, wasting time on the young."

"You're not wasting our time," said Elvis. He glanced at Amy.

Amy nodded. "Meeting you is the only good thing about this accident."

Mrs. Hunter closed her eyes. In seconds she seemed to be in a deep sleep. Elvis pulled the curtain around her bed. "She needs rest," he said in a whisper. He reached down and cupped Amy's cast in his hand. "Does it hurt?" he asked.

"Not much," said Amy. "You have to sign it. I want you to be the first."

He looked embarrassed. "You're gonna have all your friends sign it. You don't want my name there."

"I do." Amy got a pen from the table by the bed. "Sign it. I insist."

Elvis furrowed his brow as he concentrated. Then he picked up the pen. "Broken legs mend, broken hearts don't. Love, Elvis."

Amy looked down at her cast. "That's beautiful. But nobody's heart needs to be broken," she whispered.

He shook his head. Amy reached up and touched his cheek. "Don't blame yourself."

He laughed sarcastically. "Then whose fault is it?"

"Maybe nobody's. Mine, I guess, for taking the wheel. We were both acting a little crazy."

He sat down in the chair, putting the teddy bear in his arms, holding it close to his chest. His pompadour was carefully combed in front, but a lock of hair had come loose and was curling over his eye.

He was dressed in one of his weird outfits — this time black pegged pants and a pink shirt with the collar up. "It's no good, you know," he whispered, more to the teddy bear than to her.

"What?" she asked.

"Us. A girl like you has no business being with a guy like me. I'm poison to you. Look, you wound up in the hospital."

"Broken legs mend. Broken hearts don't. I read that somewhere."

"You read too much," he laughed. "It sounds like it comes from a bad song."

Amy was furious at him for laughing at his own words. "Then why did you write that?"

He shrugged. "It just came to me."

"You wrote those words because that's what you felt. But I just have a broken leg. I don't have a broken heart . . . at least not yet. Why should I? You know anybody who's planning on breaking it?"

Elvis shook his head. "Your mama and papa aren't going to ever let you see me."

"That's my problem."

"I don't think so. I don't think it's a good idea for us to see each other."

"But why?"

Elvis looked exasperated. "Look at you. Because of me you're lying in a hospital bed, my truck almost got wrecked. I could have been out of a job. My mama's furious. She says you're not the girl for me."

Amy felt something mean and angry grow in her stomach, as if screws were being tightened. What kind of mother would let her son dress the way Elvis did, without saying a word, yet tell her son that she, Amy, was bad for him?

"Me? All the parents like me. Did you tell her that I'm number one in the class?"

Elvis' eyes narrowed. Amy wished she could take the bragging words back. "She knows that," he said.

Amy paused. Elvis got a stubborn look about him when he mentioned his mother. She knew she couldn't win that battle. She decided to take another tack.

She smiled at him. She'd try teasing if anger didn't work. "Why did you come to see me with the teddy bear and sign something sweet if you wanted to just disappear into the sunset? Some friend."

"I am your friend."

"Oh yeah, that's why you'd give me a teddy bear, and then just run out on me. So I would cry on him and not you."

Elvis was so close that Amy could touch his hair. She ran her fingers along the sides, a little bit afraid to muss the careful combing.

He sat gingerly on the edge of the bed, as if afraid to get closer. Amy took his hand in hers and turned it over. She traced the life line on his palm. She had once read a book about reading palms. Carol and she had practiced on each other.

She continued to stroke his palm, tickling the area between his thumb and wrist. Carol

had a book called *Sex Without Fear* that she
had gotten from her older brother. It said
that the area between the thumb and wrist
was very sensitive.

Elvis half closed his eyes, looking content,
like a cat being stroked. Amy felt a surge of
power, so glad now that she had read that
book. Knowledge was power.

Chapter 16

The next morning, Amy's parents came to the hospital to take her home. Her father would barely look at her. Amy put on a full circle skirt that her mother had brought. It was the same one she had worn to the beauty parlor the day she met Elvis. It looked strange without any crinolines. Her leg in the cast looked huge coming out under the hem, much more ungainly-looking than it had in the hospital gown.

"I guess I won't be wearing a straight skirt for a while," Amy joked.

"You won't have to worry about what you wear," said her father. "You won't be going far."

"It was only a joke, Daddy."

"A fine time to be making jokes, young lady. I don't think you realize the seriousness of the situation."

"I do. For heaven's sake, both you and Mom act as if I broke one of your legs. I didn't do it to spite you."

"You almost got killed. You showed absolutely *no* common sense."

"And with a cracker," sniffed her mother.

Mrs. Hunter turned her head. Amy caught her eye. She was embarrassed for herself, for her parents.

"If he weren't so dirt poor, we'd sue him for every penny he had. As it is, your broken leg will cost us plenty. Don't think insurance will pay for all of it."

"I'll pay you back," said Amy.

"With what? Who knows if you'll even be able to work at that day camp this summer, and that money was supposed to go for your college."

"I'm sorry," mumbled Amy.

Mrs. Hunter shook her head. Amy remembered her words. No I'm sorrys. Well, Mrs. Hunter wasn't her mother.

"Before we leave this hospital," said her father, "I want your solemn promise that you will not see that boy."

Amy kept her head low. She saw Mrs. Hunter shake her head. "I can't promise that," said Amy.

Her father's face turned red. "You must."

Amy's lips formed a tight line. She couldn't lie.

Her mother took a step closer. "Amy, don't upset your father."

"You're both upsetting me!" cried Amy. "Look, I'm trying to be honest. It was an accident, more my fault than his. I have a right to pick my friends. He's my friend."

"You don't have that right," cried her mother. "Not if you pick the wrong people."

Amy wanted to throw her crutch.

Her father's lips were in the same thin line as Amy's. "There is nothing to discuss. If you cannot be trusted not to see that boy, then you will not go out of the house."

"Forever?" asked Amy.

"Until you come to your senses."

"Since when did this become a Communist state?" asked Amy.

"You will not talk to me like that," snapped her father. "Do you hear?"

"I hear," said Amy. "I hear."

"Now, let's go home," said her father. "You should thank God that you're coming back in one piece."

Amy sighed. Her few things were packed in a shopping bag. "I'll meet you in the hall," she said. "Just let me say good-bye to Mrs. Hunter."

"Can't you say good-bye in front of us?" asked her mother.

"She wants to say good-bye alone. It's not an act of defiance," said Mrs. Hunter. "You're going to have her alone in your home for a long time, it looks like."

Amy's mother looked hurt. "We'll wait for you in the hall. Please don't take too long. Your father has to go back to work."

Amy hobbled over to Mrs. Hunter's bed. "My parents are just upset," she said. "They have a right to be, you know. I really was to blame for the accident."

"Accidents can happen to anyone. Anyhow, you don't have to apologize to me," said Mrs. Hunter. "Remember, no I'm sorrys."

"I remember. It's just. . . . Well, I hope your hip gets better . . . and your cough."

Mrs. Hunter smiled at her. "That cough doesn't fool you, does it."

"It doesn't sound good."

"It isn't, but I'm not going yet. Don't worry."

"I'll come visit you." Amy put her crutches down gently so as not to disturb Mrs. Hunter.

"Don't make promises," said Mrs. Hunter. "You don't have to."

"What am I going to do?" sobbed Amy, suddenly breaking into tears. "My parents will kill me if I see Elvis again."

Mrs. Hunter patted her hand. "I doubt that."

"Well, I don't mean literally kill me, but — "

"You'll find a way. Just — "

"Just what?" asked Amy.

"Never mind. You have plenty of people giving you advice."

"Not like you."

"I can't tell you how to live your life. All I can tell you is to hell with protocol."

"To hell with protocol?" repeated Amy. "What does that mean?"

Mrs. Hunter laughed. "Now you've been

bragging that you're number one in the class. You're going to be a college girl. You can use words of more than one syllable. You figure it out."

Amy kissed her. Then she picked up her crutches and hopped out to her parents.

Chapter 17

Amy was miserable. Underneath the cast her leg itched unmercifully. She felt as if the hair on her leg was growing like a plant in a science-fiction movie.

Every morning she woke up hating her cast. Getting out of bed was difficult. She had to slide to the edge on her rear end and then haul herself up onto her crutches.

She got dressed. It was a beautiful, warm, sultry May day, one of the days in May when the heat was as hot as the summer, but never felt as hot because the heat was brand new.

She put on a sundress with straps that crisscrossed in the back. She was getting sick of wearing dresses with full skirts, but this dress was one that she loved.

She had mastered maneuvering on stairs with her crutches. She hardly faltered as she went down the stairs.

Her father was eating breakfast alone, reading the newspaper. "Where's Mom?" Amy asked.

"She's on the phone. Aunt Sarabeth. You know. . . ." Her father made a quacking motion with his hand. He smiled at Amy.

Amy didn't smile back. During the time that she had been home, it was as if war had been declared between her father and herself. The broken leg was a war wound. Amy was a prisoner of war, and she was refusing to collaborate with the enemy.

Her father sighed. "How long are you going to keep this up?"

"Pardon me?" asked Amy in her most icily polite tone.

Her father crumbled the paper. "I would like for once to be spoken to in a decent tone of voice."

"Yes, sir," said Amy, keeping her tone even. She kept her head high. She wanted so badly to crumble, to tell her father that she loved him and that everything was fine. The truth was that she did not even understand why she still felt so angry at him.

Rationally, she had to admit that her parents had a right to be upset with her, even to punish her. She had endangered her life. She had lied to them. All the things they had warned her about she had done.

"Have it your own way," said her father. "Someday, you're going to regret the pain you're causing."

"Yes, sir."

"Please stop calling me sir."

"I only meant it as a sign of respect, sir."

Her father glared at her. Her mother came

into the kitchen. Unlike her father, Amy's mother had refused to admit that anything had changed. She acted as if Amy's tone of voice was entirely proper and normal, and nothing Amy could say could shake her unfailing necessity to keep things "nice." As far as her mother was concerned the broken leg was like a little "flu" that Amy had mysteriously caught. The rebellion behind it was ignored.

Her father left the room, leaving Amy alone with her mother. "I wish you wouldn't upset your father," she said.

"I have kept to the letter of my punishment," said Amy. "I have not violated the rules you set down."

"I know, honey. That's not it. But you haven't said a civil word to him in a week."

Or to you, Amy thought to herself.

"I have answered when spoken to." Amy spoke in the voice she had perfected — the voice of a robot.

"You know, your father is a very sensitive man," said her mother. "I know you don't mean this. But he's frightened."

Amy stared at her mother. Frightened! Her father frightened by her? She had never considered it.

"We have to go out this evening," said her mother. "I hope you'll be all right. I'm leaving you some cold chicken."

Amy's heart pounded. This would be the first time that her parents were leaving her alone. She *had* to see Elvis. Her parents had forbidden her to go out, but she had not promised not to see Elvis again. She would be sticking to the letter of her punishment if she allowed him in the house. She was determined to find some way to at least talk to Elvis. She felt as if she couldn't live without him. But he didn't even have a phone. She had no way of getting in touch with him, and he hadn't even tried to get in touch with her.

As soon as her parents left the house, she called Carol. "I need your help. You've got to go to Elvis' house right away. It's crucial. Tell him it's safe for him to come over tonight."

Amy could hear Carol sigh over the telephone. "Oh no. Amy, your parents will kill you. Besides, I thought your romance with the frog prince was over."

"Very funny. Will you go to Elvis' house for me? They don't have a phone."

"Amy, I don't know — "

"What's the problem?" snapped Amy. "I've helped you and Steve out countless times. This is only the second time I've asked you for help."

"Yes, but I have all my limbs intact."

"Carol . . . please. I haven't heard from Elvis since I left the hospital. I'm sure he's worried about me, but there's been no way for me to get in touch with him. I need you."

"Okay, Amy. You win. I'm sorry. If you like him so much, there must be something more to him. I'll give him your message."

Amy closed her eyes for a second. "Thanks," she whispered.

Amy hung up the phone and prayed that Elvis would be at home. What if Carol couldn't find him? What if she *did* find him and he didn't want to come over? Amy practically drove herself crazy worrying. She turned on the radio to WHBQ, Elvis' favorite station. Just listening to the music he loved made her miss him even more.

She heard a soft knock at the door. She got her crutches and hopped over. She opened the door. Elvis was standing there.

"Hi," he said softly.

Amy wanted to fling her arms around him. "Hi! You made it!"

"Carol came over and told me you had to see me right away."

"God, I owe her my life. Come on in."

Elvis hesitated on the porch. He had all his weight on one foot. His left leg shook nervously. "Ahh . . . I don't know if I should."

"Why?"

"Well, your parents . . . if they found out, they'd kill me. I just came by to see you. . . . I — "

"Come in," she insisted. "It's all right. They forbade me to go out with you, but they didn't say anything about having you in."

Elvis frowned. "It's still not right."

Amy put the crutch under her armpit and grabbed him. "Come in!" she said. She pulled with such force that she threw her weight off balance.

Elvis caught her. "Will you be careful! You've got a broken leg, you know."

Amy looked down at her cast. "So that's what it is. I thought I was just gaining lopsided weight. I thought my leg looked funny."

Elvis closed the door behind him. "You are crazy. You know that?"

"I'm not crazy." Amy let her crutches fall. She put her arms around Elvis' neck.

He picked her up and carried her to the couch, carefully supporting her cast. Then he went back to the hallway and got her crutches. Carefully he rested them on an armchair. He sat on the edge of the couch. He looked out of place among all the stuffed furniture. It looked too soft for him. He studied her. "You are crazy."

Amy was annoyed. "I wish you'd stop saying that. I'm crazy about you. That doesn't make me crazy."

"Same difference."

"It is not. Haven't you ever heard of animal magnetism?"

"I don't know of any animal that would be talkin' like you with a cast on its leg. If an animal got hurt it would have the sense to stay away from the one who hurt it."

Amy threw back her head. She started to howl loudly.

"What are you doing?"

"I decided that if you're going to keep calling me crazy, I'll act crazy." She giggled.

Elvis laughed.

"Give in," said Amy. "Admit that I'm not crazy."

He nodded. "I give in."

Amy looked over at him. "Does that mean that you can give me a kiss?"

He leaned over her and supported his body with his arms, taking care not to put any weight on her. She felt fragile and cared for.

Amy clung to him, pulling him tighter. She could feel his chest against her body.

His hands were under her sweater, rubbing the small of her back. She knew that Carol always let Steve undo her bra when they made out.

Elvis drew back. His eyes wouldn't let her look away. He looked tender and soft.

Amy put her arms around him again. "It's okay," she said.

His arms were around her again. This time she felt him fumbling with the hooks in her bra. His fingernails were digging into her back, and she couldn't concentrate on the kiss. She wanted to tell him that he was hurting her, but she was afraid to break the mood.

Finally he got the last hook loose. He didn't bring his hands around to her breasts. He just kept rubbing her back and kissing her.

Then slowly his left hand came around to the front. Amy could barely swallow. Her eyes were open, looking at him so close.

He groaned. His fingers touched the edge of her breast.

"You're so beautiful."

Amy stifled an urge to answer, No, I'm not.

Then his hand moved again, and Amy stiffened. She was scared to let him go further. Would he think she was too easy?

As soon as he felt her pull away, Elvis sat up.

"Sorry," he mumbled. But he sounded angry.

"No . . . sorrys. . . . It's just. . . ."

Amy half sat up. The damned cast made her feel so awkward. She kept trying to sit up and falling back onto the pillows. Then she started to laugh.

"What's so funny?"

Amy got herself into a sitting position. She scratched Elvis' back. "I think I'm just nervous. I just thought a girl's supposed to remember the first time she's touched . . . you know. But I'm the only one I know who'll have a cast to remember it by."

"I didn't hurt you, did I?"

"Uh . . . uh."

He looked at her. Then they both laughed.

"It's stupid to be this nervous," Amy said.

Elvis studied the pattern in the oriental carpet. Amy rubbed his back.

"It's not that I didn't like it," she said. She wished now that she hadn't stopped him.

"Do you have anything to eat?" he asked abruptly. "I'm hungry."

"Hungry?"

"Food, you know." He made munching noises, then pulled Amy's nose.

Amy rubbed it. He had pulled hard.

She got her crutches and went into the kitchen. Her bra felt strange, its ends flapping under her sweater.

He ate the cold chicken and potato salad and half the blueberry pie. Amy wondered how she was going to explain to her parents that she had gone on an eating binge. But she loved having him there, across the kitchen table. If only her parents would never come home.

Finally he stopped. He grinned at Amy. "Your mama's a good cook."

"I love you," Amy said in a half whisper.

Elivs looked up abruptly. He gave her a slow grin. Then he stood up. "I gotta go. Your parents might come back and they'll kill us."

"Elvis, I just said, I love you. You can't just ignore that I said it."

He winked at her.

"What does that mean?" Amy demanded, furious.

"Hey, don't get all upset. I love you, too." He threw the words away as if they didn't mean anything. "Hey, you know what I did the other day?"

Amy looked down at the dirty plates. She didn't care what he did the other day. She felt as if they were two planets in different orbits.

"Hey," he said, sounding annoyed. "Don't you care?"

Amy shrugged.

"I went to this little place I knew about. I just wanted to hear what I sounded like. It only cost four bucks. I made a record. What a joke. I sounded like somebody beating on a bucket lid. But the lady there, she was a secretary or something . . . she took my name. . . . Ain't that something?"

Amy barely heard his words. All she could remember was the tone of his voice when he had said I love you, too, as if he couldn't wait to get rid of the words.

She got her crutches and hopped to the door. "Next week I get my cast off. I'll be able to get outside more."

He seemed distracted. "That's good."

"So, I'll see you?" Amy couldn't help but make it a question.

"Yeah . . . but Amy, we can't get too hot and heavy. . . . Your parents — "

"It's a little too late for that, isn't it?"

Elvis shrugged again. She was beginning to hate that shrug. Hate it with a passion. She wished she had never told him she loved him.

Chapter 18

The cast on Amy's leg was finally coming off for good. Amy sat in the backseat of the family car, her leg stretched out before her. She looked at the many signatures on the cast — Carol's cute drawing of an elephant with its trunk in a cast. But the one signature that stood out was Elvis', the loop of the L much larger than the E. The handwriting slanted up, but it was neat and easy to read. Beside his name was the heart, a small one — "Broken legs mend, broken hearts don't."

Amy wondered if she'd be able to keep the cast. She would have to tell the doctor to please not cut through Elvis' signature.

Her father helped her out of the car. He held her hand for a second longer than necessary. Their eyes met.

Amy smiled at him. "Thanks, Dad," she said softly.

He broke out into a wide grin. "I bet it feels good to be getting that thing off." His words rushed together. Amy felt sorry for him. She was shocked to realize that one smile from her could mean so much.

"It does," admitted Amy. "I'll feel about ten pounds lighter." She kept her voice light, too, a gift that she realized she could make to her father without losing too much.

She took her crutches and swung through the parking lot and up the hospital steps.

She was a little bit afraid that the doctor would hurt her when he took the cast off. He had told her that he took it off with an electric saw. She envisioned the saw missing and going straight through her limb.

She sat up on the doctor's table. He brought out the saw. "Wait!" shouted Amy. "Can I keep it?"

"Keep what?" asked the doctor.

"The cast." She pointed to Elvis's signature. "I want you to save that."

"Your boyfriend?" asked the doctor in a teasing voice.

Amy looked at her father. "A friend," she said.

The doctor sighed. "Girls. . . . I'll try, but I make no guarantee." Within seconds, her cast lay on the table, split in two.

Amy picked it up. The doctor had sawed through "Broken legs mend, broken hearts don't." She put the two halves together. She'd keep them both.

She looked down at her exposed leg — pale, almost yellow-looking, with thick, black stubble on it.

"Yuk."

The doctor laughed. "Teenage girls. At least most of the hair rubbed off under the cast. I bet you expected a jungle growth."

"I did, but it's still disgusting!"

The doctor ran his hands along her calf. Her leg was both scrawny and flabby, a particularly revolting combination.

She stood up. She felt vulnerable without the cast, as if armor had been removed. She tried taking a few steps. Her leg felt wobbly, but the knee bent. It seemed to have a better memory of how to walk than she did.

"How does it feel?" asked the doctor.

"Okay, I guess. Weak."

"That's natural. You lost almost fifty percent of your muscle tone in the first few days. I'm going to give you a set of exercises you should do to strengthen it, and I'll want to see you again in two weeks. It won't take long to gain your full strength back."

Amy looked doubtful.

"Trust me," said the doctor.

Her mother smiled at the doctor. Amy felt a little less trusting.

"How long before it gets back to normal?" Amy asked.

"That depends on you. Are sports important to you?"

"I like to play baseball. And I have a job lined up this summer as a day-camp counselor."

"You should be fine. *If* you do the exercises. Don't worry."

"She won a scholarship to a college prep

program at Tennessee State," said her mother proudly.

"Well, she shouldn't have any trouble at all this fall. She can join the football team if she wants." The doctor laughed heartily. Amy didn't feel like laughing. Just returning to the hospital depressed her.

"Well, dear, I think we should thank the doctor and we should leave." Her mother spoke in a sugary tone that grated. Amy stared down at the hair on her sickly looking leg. "I'd like to go see Mrs. Hunter," she said. "Just see how she is."

"She's not well, I'm afraid," said the doctor. "I don't think that's a good idea. Her cough has gotten worse. I'm sorry." The doctor looked over Amy's head to her father. He shook his head.

Amy wondered if Mrs. Hunter was dying. But even if she was, why did the doctor think that she shouldn't see her?

"Please," pleaded Amy. "I'd like to see her. I'll just say hello."

"I think it will be distressing for you, darling," said her father.

All the darlings and sweethearts were driving Amy crazy. She wanted to scream.

"Please," repeated Amy, but this time there was no pleading in her voice.

The doctor shrugged his shoulders.

"She is my friend," said Amy.

The silence in the doctor's office was made all the more noticeable by the sounds of the hospital in the corridor. Finally her mother gave in. "Have it your own way," she sniffed. "But your father has to get back to work. I hope you don't stay long."

Amy walked through the hospital corridors without crutches. The distances that had seemed so vast now just took seconds. She turned the corner and remembered the day that she had looked up and seen Elvis, standing with the teddy bear in his arms.

She walked into her old room. The curtains were pulled around Mrs. Hunter's bed. Amy's old bed was empty, the sheets pulled so tight that it looked as if nobody had ever been there. Amy felt a shiver. The bed looked as if someone might have died. She remembered that the woman who had used the bed before her *had* died.

She pulled aside the curtains to Mrs. Hunter's bed. Mrs. Hunter looked shriveled. Tubes were coming out of her nose and she was making a terrible rasping noise that sounded inhuman. An IV was dripping fluid into her vein, but she looked as if she weighed less than fifty pounds.

Amy sat down beside her. She had never seen anyone dying before. She was curious that Mrs. Hunter had lived even this long. When you read about someone dying, it always seemed like it happened fast. But Mrs. Hunter had looked like she was dying a month ago when Amy was in the hospital with her. Now, here she was still alive, still attached to tubes, but not dead yet. Her hand was warm, full of life.

Amy lay her cheek against Mrs. Hunter's hand. She stroked it, the way she had Elvis' hand. "I hope you're dreaming wonderful dreams," whispered Amy. "Of all those handsome men who loved you."

"Made love to me," whispered Mrs. Hunter. "Sex. It's not a dirty word."

Amy looked up, startled. Mrs. Hunter's eyes were still closed.

Mrs. Hunter cackled. "A dying woman says the word sex, and everyone's shocked."

"Mrs. Hunter . . . it's me, Amy."

"I know," whispered Mrs. Hunter.

Amy wasn't at all sure that Mrs. Hunter did know, but she continued to stroke her hand.

"I'm sorry I haven't visited you before," said Amy. "I couldn't. My parents have forbidden me to go anywhere. But today I came to have my cast taken off."

Mrs. Hunter turned. Her eyes opened. "Your parents are assholes."

Amy gasped. She pulled her hand away and put both her hands primly in her lap.

"The only good thing about dying is that you can tell people whatever you want."

"I don't think that living ever stopped you," said Amy bitterly. "You shouldn't have called my parents that. It isn't nice."

Mrs. Hunter laughed. It was a genuine laugh, not a cackle. "You're right. Now don't get all huffy on me. I know how hard it is to admit that your relatives are assholes. Imagine what it's like having to admit that your own children are." She lay her head back down.

Amy refused to feel sorry for her. "Then stop using that word."

"I can't. I've been planning for years that it's gonna be my dying word."

"Then don't say it," said Amy fiercely. "I don't want you to die. 'Do not go gentle into that good night . . . rage, rage against the dying of the light.' "

"What are you talking about?"

"That's from my favorite Dylan Thomas poem. He wrote it about his father."

Mrs. Hunter sniffed. "That's a young person's poem anyhow. How old was the guy who wrote that?"

"I don't know, but he died last year when he was only thirty-nine. He was an alcoholic."

"There you have it. I never knew a drunk who could look death in the face."

"I won't be able to stand it if you die. Don't you dare die while I'm here."

Mrs. Hunter laughed again. "That's my Amy. Egotistical to the end."

"I don't mean to be egotistical," said Amy. Amy was seized with the desire to get away. She felt ashamed of her legs, whole now. She could walk out of here. Mrs. Hunter would never get out of bed. Never. She would die alone.

"Don't you dare pity me," Mrs. Hunter's voice snapped. She closed her eyes again.

"Go out and say good-bye to that young man of yours."

"He's not exactly *my* young man. I've only seen him once when my parents were out. I'm not sure how much he really cares."

"Idiot," whispered Mrs. Hunter.

"Him or me?"

"You. Don't look surprised. That boy needs you. Oh, not forever, but you go and tell him that he's smart, not dumb. You go tell him that those are a dying woman's words. He needs to hear them."

Amy wanted to cry. "What about me?"

"What about you? All your life you've been told you're smart, right?"

Amy nodded.

"All your life you've been told you're a good girl, right?"

Amy nodded.

"Well, you need me to tell you that you're also an asshole. But you're not an assaholic. Those are people addicted to being idiots. There's hope for you. It doesn't have to be hereditary."

"My parents aren't bad." Amy felt defensive.

Mrs. Hunter sighed. "No, but they're scared, and you want more than that. That's why you saw something in that boy. But he's not as strong as you. You saw that, too, but you don't want to look at that. I'm getting tired."

Amy stood up. She was about to leave

when she stopped and leaned over the bed, afraid that she would dislodge one of the tubes. She kissed Mrs. Hunter on the cheek. She saw tears in the corners of Mrs. Hunter's eyes.

"You're not an asshole," Mrs. Hunter whispered. And then she closed her eyes.

Amy stood there for a second. She saw out of the corner of her eye a woman about her mother's age standing in the doorway of the hospital room. The woman looked uncertain whether she could come in.

"I'm just leaving," said Amy.

"Who are you?" asked the woman, emphasizing the word *you*.

Amy introduced herself and explained that she had shared the room with Mrs. Hunter for just a night.

"I'm her daughter," said the woman. She looked at her mother. "She looks like she's resting. I'll let her sleep."

"She was awake," Amy started to say, but the woman had already left the room.

Amy followed her. "I'm sorry your mother's so sick," said Amy. "She's a wonderful woman."

The woman sighed. "She's been sick for so long. It's awful for her. If only she would go . . . it would be a blessing."

Amy wanted to scream NO!

"It would be for the best," repeated Mrs. Hunter's daughter.

"No . . . no. . . . Dead . . . it's not for the best," stammered Amy.

The woman stared at her. "I beg your pardon. You don't have to sit here and watch her suffer."

Amy glared at her. Asshole, she thought to herself. Then she left to join her own parents.

Chapter 19

Amy lay in the backyard. Her leg was stronger, and tan, thanks to Carol's insistence that she immediately sun herself. Amy took a drink of ice tea as she sunned herself.

How could Elvis not call her? School was out. She was about to start day camp. It had been weeks since he had last seen her. How could he kiss her like that and then just disappear? Was he *that* afraid of her parents? Then she remembered Mrs. Hunter's message to him. "Tell him he's smart. Tell him he's not dumb." She had an excuse to go see him. She had a message for him.

She walked to Elvis' home. She would see him today, no matter what. Elvis lived behind the Lauderdale Courts housing project. Amy knew that Elvis had lived in the projects when he went to high school, but now that he was earning money, he and his parents had been able to move into a two-story house on Alabama Street, renting the ground floor.

As she got closer, Amy got a little fright-

ened. She had never met his family, although
he had talked about them enough, especially
his mother.

A lady was sitting on the front porch. She
was short and plump with flabby arms. Her
hair was done in tight curls above her broad
forehead. She had at least two chins, if
not more, but her eyes had a dreamy look
to them. In fact, she looked happy and lost in
a daydream. Amy knew she was Elvis'
mother, just from the eyes.

"Excuse me. Is Elvis here?" Amy asked.

"What do you want with him?"

"I'm his friend, Amy Klinger."

The dreamy look left, and her eyes got
smaller and meaner. "You're the girl who
got him in the accident."

"We were in that together," Amy said
bravely. "I've got to talk to him."

"He told me your parents didn't want you
to see him no more. That you were too good
for him."

"That's not true."

"What's not?" asked his mother shrewdly.
"That you're too good for him or that your
parents won't let you see him?"

"The first," Amy admitted.

"Well, at least you're honest. But I don't
want you getting my boy in trouble."

"I won't. I just want to talk to him."

"He's not here."

"Where is he? Will he be back soon?"

Elvis' mother looked as if she didn't want
to answer her.

"Please," pleaded Amy. "I really am his friend."

Elvis' mother got a dreamy look in her eyes again. She was looking at something beyond Amy.

Amy turned around. Elvis was standing on the sidewalk, carrying a brown paper bag full of groceries.

"Hi," she said shyly.

He didn't answer. Instead he looked up at his mother. "Is anything wrong, Ma?" he asked.

His mother shook her head, but her lips were tightly closed. "I don't know what she wants."

"I want to talk," said Amy. "I don't mean any harm."

"That doesn't mean you won't do any," said Elvis' mother.

Elvis stood silently, letting his mother and Amy talk around him.

"I haven't done any harm," Amy protested. "That's not fair. You can't blame me for liking Elvis."

Elvis' mother got a sly smile on her face. "You're not so dumb. For a smart girl. Dinner's ready soon. Elvis, you can talk to her if you want, but don't go far."

Amy looked down the steps at Elvis. He was staring at the ground, his weight on one hip, trying to look as if what the two women in his life talked about didn't matter.

His mother got up and went inside.

Amy turned and faced Elvis. "How do you like me on two legs?"

Elvis looked at her legs. "They look pretty good. How are you?"

"Okay . . . but I thought I'd hear from you."

Elvis studied the sidewalk. He shrugged.

"Look at me, damn it," Amy snapped. "I'm risking a lot to come here, and you act as if the sidewalk's more interesting."

Elvis looked around to see if anybody was listening to her. "We've got neighbors, you know. And my mama's just inside. I don't want her to think I know girls who swear."

"Heaven help me," said Amy. "That should be the worst thing. Everybody's got neighbors and mothers."

"I don't like to hear girls swear."

"I'm sorry, but you'd better pay attention to me."

"Every time I do, there's trouble."

"You know that's not true."

"You know it is."

Amy sighed. She walked down the steps. She put her arm around his and led him down the sidewalk. "Can we go for a walk? Let's go to the river. The fair will be starting soon."

He smiled at her. "You sure don't take no for an answer." They walked to the river, barely talking.

Finally Amy broke the silence. "I've been thinking about us a lot. I think we have a lot in common."

"You and I are so different I can't count the ways. You come from a family with money."

"Not mine. My uncle's."

"Same thing."

"It isn't. Can't you see anything beyond your nose? Can you imagine how Dad feels clerking in my uncle's drugstore? How would you like to be the one everyone pities?" Her voice caught. "I think my father hates his life. He's sad all the time, and there's nothing I can do about it."

Elvis just looked at her. They reached the river. The carnival was about to begin. The carnival people had already begun to set up their tents. Amy could see their trailers parked haphazardly along the river, as if thrown up by a flood.

She had always loved the carnival, even though her mother said the carnival people were dirty. She loved the rides and the feeling of freedom wandering around, the feeling that anything could happen.

Elvis led her down to the park, holding her hand chivalrously. "Your leg really doesn't bother you?"

Amy shook her head. "No, it just feels weak. I do exercises for it. I'm going to start work at the day camp next week. I keep thinking it's gonna buckle under me, but it seems to work okay. I'm glad you didn't see it when the cast first came off. It was disgusting. Yellow and flabby. It's still pretty flabby."

"Do you think that would have bothered me?"

"Yeah, you're pretty fussy. You're always clean. You may dress a little weird, but you're clean."

"Yeah, I can just see that on my gravestone. 'He was weird but clean.'"

"That's not what's gonna be on your gravestone."

"Oh yeah, maybe you should pitch a tent here. 'Amy Klinger Predicts Your Gravestone! Twenty-five cents.'"

"I wouldn't want to do that. I think people care too much about what's written on their graves. It's what happens when we're alive that counts. When you're dead, you're dead. Just rot. You can't live for your tombstone."

"Hey . . . no reason to get morbid."

"I'm not being morbid."

"I don't like talk about graves and gravestones." His voice sounded harsh. "You don't know anything about death."

"What do you mean?"

"Nothing."

"Nobody spits those words out and means nothing."

"It's just I've *lived* with death my whole life."

Amy didn't understand. "Both your parents are alive."

Elvis had dropped her hand. "Forget it."

"No, we can't be friends unless we tell each other what we feel. You can't do that to friends."

"I don't have friends."

"I'm your friend. I don't know why. It's like we were twins or something. Ever since we met, you've just been important to me."

At the word *twin* Elvis stiffened. "Don't say that," he hissed.

"It's what I feel. I feel like we're twins. Oh, I know we don't look alike. But I feel like inside, we're alike."

Elvis' face had grown pale.

"Are you a witch? Do you want to die?" Elvis turned and grabbed her arms above the elbow. He was squeezing hard. "Did you know? Are you making fun of me?"

"What are you talking about?"

"My twin."

"What twin?"

"I was born a twin. My brother died at birth. We were identical. Look, I can prove it."

Elvis sat down on the grass and took off one of his shoes and socks. "Look at this." He pointed to his toes. The second and third toes were webbed together, joined by a thin, almost translucent layer of skin.

Amy sat down on the grass and looked at it curiously.

It didn't disgust her. She put out her hand to touch it. Elvis pushed her hand away from his foot. "It's a sign," he said. "A sign that my baby brother lives in me. All his life force went into me when he died. That's why I'm special."

"That's not why you're special," whispered Amy, looking at the deformed toes. It wasn't disgusting at all, just strange.

But Elvis didn't even seem to hear her. "My mama couldn't have babies after me . . . so it's like all the life force from all the babies she might have had is in me, too."

Amy stroked his arm. He seemed so lost.

Elvis shook his head. He put his sock back on his foot. "So now you know my secret. You can't be my twin. I already have one. He's up there in heaven, looking out for me."

Amy plucked out a blade of grass. "Do you remember that lady in the hospital, Mrs. Hunter? I went to see her. She's dying."

"I'm surprised she lived this long. That lady looked like she was dying a month ago."

"She's not a lady, that's why I like her. In some ways, I like her even more than my own mama. I mean, I love my mama, but I like Mrs. Hunter. Mrs. Hunter sees the real me."

Elvis frowned at her. "You shouldn't talk that way about your mama."

"Well, it's not that I don't love my mama. It's just that my mother wants me to play it so safe."

"What's wrong with that? Your mama just wants what's best for you."

Elvis sounded so much like a little boy. Amy looked at him. She felt sad. She touched his arm. "Forget what I said. I came to give you a message from Mrs. Hunter."

"That old witch talked about me?"

"Stop calling her a witch. She's great. She told me to tell you that you were smart."

Elvis laughed so loudly that he started to snort. "Smart . . . well there you have it."

"She meant it. You are. I know you are, too. You're just smart about yourself, but she said you don't believe in yourself, and you should."

"Yeah . . . well, she must be brilliant. She's ending up dying alone in the hospital."

"That's not her fault."

"I don't like this talk about dying." Elvis stood up. "I gotta get home for dinner with Mama. You'd better get home, too."

"Elvis. . . ." Amy wasn't sure what she wanted. Elvis looked uncomfortable.

"Go home," said Elvis. "And stop talking nonsense about your parents."

"Shut up," Amy snapped. "Now you listen to me. You're smart and you're special, and not because of any mumbo-jumbo about a dead twin. But you'd better stop feeling sorry for yourself, 'cause that's going to get you in trouble!"

"Shut up. You are a witch. I have a dream all the time and I wake up screaming shut up."

"What happens in your dream?"

"I'm surrounded by men who want to hurt me." Elvis' voice was so low, Amy could hardly hear him.

"I'm sorry I shouted shut up at you," she said.

Elvis shrugged.

"Come on," said Elvis harshly. "You gotta get home. I gotta get home for dinner."

Amy shrugged herself. But the shrug depressed her.

Chapter 20

Elvis was dressed in a pink suit with white shoes. He practically shone in the sunlight outside of Easton's Beauty Salon. The suit looked as if it had been designed never to see daylight. He grinned at both Amy and her mother. "Amy, I've got to talk to you. I've got news."

Amy's mother grabbed her hand. "You will not speak to that boy," she hissed.

Amy had never seen Elvis look so excited. She broke away from her mother. "I've got to talk to him, Ma. Look at him. He's bursting about something."

"I'm glad your father's not here," said her mother, but she walked on into Easton's.

Amy ran across the street to Elvis. "What's up?"

Elvis nodded. "I forgot your mom came, too. I thought you'd be alone."

"That's okay. Now tell me, what's the big news?" Elvis just grinned wider. He licked his lips. He put his hands in the low pockets of his pleated pants and leaned against a car.

Amy burst out laughing. "Are you gonna make me strangle you to get your news?"

"Okay. Okay. . . . I told you I paid four bucks to hear myself sing. Well, that guy at Sun, he called. It was weird. But he wants me to work with a band. Wants me to practice. Maybe he wants me to make a record."

Amy threw her arms around his neck and kissed him hard on the lips. Elvis looked embarrassed. "We're right on the street."

"Who cares?"

"I do," said Elvis. He straightened his shirt. "I told Mr. Phillips I need a band, and he gave me the name of this guy. I'm supposed to meet him this afternoon. His name's Scotty Moore. He's older. He works at a dry-cleaning plant and he's married."

"You nervous?"

"Me, nah."

"You are. . . . Do you want me to come with you?"

"You can't. Your mama won't let you." Elvis had a pleading tone in his voice. Amy knew he was scared. She had to go with him.

She lifted up on her tiptoes and kissed him on the cheek. "Don't worry." She went inside the beauty parlor. Easton was combing her mother's wet hair.

"I saw you out the window," said her mother. "How could you kiss that boy in broad daylight?"

"That's what he asked, too."

Easton giggled.

"Mom, I've got to talk to you."

Mrs. Klinger looked around the beauty parlor. "Not here."

"Easton doesn't mind. It's appropriate. I met Elvis here. He wants me to go with him this afternoon. He needs me. It's nothing romantic. I'll be back by dinner. I don't want to lie to you."

"You can't. We forbid you to see him."

"Mom, it's not even a date. He's actually going to make a record. He's scared and I want to go with him."

"That guy sings, too? I didn't know that," exclaimed Easton. "I thought all he did was dress funny."

Amy's mother's lips tightened. "I don't know what I'll tell your father."

"Why tell him anything?" asked Easton.

"Do you think I should just let her go?" Amy's mother asked Easton.

"He's not a bad boy. He's always polite. Besides, I don't know how you're going to stop her."

Amy smiled. "Thanks," she whispered.

Her mother sighed. "Well, as long as it's not a real date."

Amy winked at Easton. Then she ran out of the shop and across the street to Elvis. "Can you wait an hour while I have my hair done?"

"Yeah . . . we don't have to be there till two. But is your ma letting you go with me?"

Amy nodded. "Just let anybody try to stop me. I'll see you in an hour."

An hour later, driving with Elvis, Amy sat as close to him as she could. He kept both hands on the wheel. He had that same look of concentration that he had at the gospel sing. Occasionally he would flip the radio dial as if he couldn't find any station that satisfied him.

"You're going to be fine," said Amy. "That guy wouldn't have asked you to make a record if he didn't think you were good."

"Oh yeah, you know what he liked about me? He thought I sounded like a Negro."

Amy was shocked.

Elvis glanced at her. "That's right. He said that if he could find a white boy who could sing like a Negro, he'd make a million, and he thought I was the one."

"You don't sound Negro. You sound — I don't know."

Elvis sighed. "I don't know, either. Probably this guy, Scotty Moore, will think I sound like a sick cat."

"Nope. You don't sound like a sick cat. I can guarantee that."

Elvis started to laugh.

Amy put her arm around his neck. She kissed him lightly. "Relax, you're going to be terrific."

They pulled up to a small house on Betz Street.

"Is this the place?"

"Yeah." It was more of a cough than a

word. He was so nervous that he could hardly speak.

Amy watched as Elvis got out of the driver's seat and headed straight for the front door, forgetting all about her. She opened the car door for herself and followed him up to the front porch.

Scotty Moore and his wife both answered the door. Scotty looked older, with a long, lean face and a hooked nose like a hawk. He greeted Elvis warmly, but Scotty's wife looked as if she wanted to run out the back door when she saw Elvis' ducktail, pink suit, and white shoes. She could barely extend her hand to shake Elvis'. It was as if she thought he had a disease.

"How do you do, ma'am?" mumbled Elvis in his most polite voice.

Amy shook her hand, too. Mrs. Moore seemed a little reassured. If Elvis was with someone as normal as Amy, he might not be all weird. Amy was glad that she came.

Scotty took Elvis into the back room where he had set up a microphone and an amplifier for an electric guitar. Bill Black, a next-door neighbor, came in. He played the stand-up base. He was a big man with a quick smile, but both men looked as if they were in their twenties. Amy knew that Elvis felt out of place.

Amy and Scotty's wife sat in the back of the room while Elvis, Scotty, and Bill went through some old songs. Elvis sounded tight and nervous, not the way he sounded when he relaxed. He was so polite to the others that his voice never rose above a mumble.

Amy smiled at him, hoping that he'd relax and stop treating the other two musicians as if they were teachers who were about to give him a bad grade.

They tried every variety of songs. They ran through Marty Robbins, Billy Eckstine, the Inkspots, almost every song they knew. Amy could tell that Scotty and Bill didn't think Elvis was great.

Finally, they took a break. Elvis was sweating. Huge half moons stained the underarms of his new shirt. The pink pants were wrinkled and looked as if he had tried to sleep in them.

He came over and poured himself a glass of ice tea. "Pretty awful, isn't it?"

Amy shook her head. She looked across the room. Scotty and the bass player were whispering together. Elvis followed her glance. "Probably looking for a way to politely get rid of me," mumbled Elvis. "They're professionals. I'm strictly amateur."

"No," said Amy. "But — "

"But what?" Elvis asked.

"Stop being so polite. You're not as polite as all that!"

Elvis stared at her. "What do you mean?"

"When you get scared you get all polite, but sometimes I just wish you'd fight back. Tell everybody to shut the hell up and just listen to you sing."

"You're sure one polite girl," said Elvis sarcastically.

"Well, it takes one to know one. Trust me. Don't be polite. As a great lady said, 'To hell with protocol.' Start foolin' around. You're always better when you fool around."

Amy surprised herself by how loudly she had talked. Bill and Scotty looked up. Then they all started to laugh.

"Your girl friend might have some good advice."

Amy expected Elvis to say she wasn't his girl friend. But he just grinned at her. "Don't mind her. She always likes to tell me what to do."

"Well, listen to her," said Scotty. He picked up his guitar.

They started in again. This time Elvis couldn't seem to stand still. He threw his head to one side and looked at Amy sideways, giving her a sarcastic leer. His hands swung up with the beat.

His knees bent. His left leg shook and swiveled. He sent Amy a wicked, teasing grin. Then his whole body seemed to shake with the chorus. He stuck his pelvis out and back, each time shaking his head with the same teasing smile.

Amy started to laugh. Her hand went up to her mouth. She watched him swivel and turn, flying around the little room, his hips going back and forth, back and forth.

With each line, he stopped for just a fraction of a second, and flashed the same half-sarcastic, foolin'-around smile.

Amy laughed so hard she wanted to scream. Then she wasn't laughing anymore. She wanted to explode.

His voice went low and high, as if he were singing all the harmonies with himself, slurring some of the words, singing the other ones oddly, all alone, dancing and singing all alone.

"What're you doing?" yelled Amy when he finished.

Elvis just laughed. "I can't help but move to it. I can't help it. I can't sit still."

"Don't! Don't!" yelled Amy. "Don't stand still!"

"I can't do that at the audition. He'll kick me out. He'll hate it."

"No, he won't!" shouted Amy. "Nobody will hate it. Don't worry!"

Chapter 21

It was one of the hottest Julys on record. At
day camp, Amy had kept her kids in the lake
until they came out looking like prunes. Amy
had been kicked in the face almost a hundred
times as she tried to teach her group to float,
but it was worth it. At least they had stayed
cool.

Now, on the bus coming home, Amy felt as
if she was melting. The temperature hit one
hundred and wouldn't leave. She couldn't
believe that little kids still had energy to
sing, much less make it all the way through
"One Hundred Bottles of Beer on the Wall."
They were driving her crazy.

Finally she saw the last kid off the bus.
Matthew, the bus driver, smiled at her.
"Looks like it's gonna be another scorcher
tomorrow, and it's only Wednesday," he said.

Amy gave him a wilted smile. He had been
flirting with her all summer, but she hadn't
paid too much attention to him. Now she
gave him a second glance. He had freckles

and curly red hair. He grinned at her. "Don't melt," he said.

Amy laughed. "You be careful, too," she said. She swung off the bus. Her legs were tanned a deep brown. She was wearing a madras halter and white shorts.

When she got in the house, her mother was sitting in front of the fan in the kitchen, snapping the ends of green beans. Amy gave her a kiss and picked up a green bean. She ate it raw.

"That'll give you a stomachache," warned her mother.

Amy didn't answer. She sat down and began helping her mother with the beans.

"You had a phone call," said her mother.

Something in her mother's voice made Amy wary. "Who was it?" she asked.

"It was that boy! He said to tell you to listen to WHBQ tonight. He said it was important. Probably some radio promotion. He couldn't even leave a number for you to call him back. I asked. Some manners. He just said to give you the message, and then he hung up."

"I bet he's going to be on the air. I bet it's his record. And he couldn't leave a number because they don't have a phone."

"Crackers," said her mother.

Amy flashed her mother a dirty look. She got up from the table and brought her mother a box of saltines. "Here you are," she said politely, grabbing another green bean and eating it rather loudly.

Her mother took a cracker without saying another word.

After dinner, Amy excused herself and started to go upstairs to her bedroom.

"Where are you going?" asked her father. "It's too early to go to sleep."

"I'm tired," said Amy. "It's been so hot. The kids are driving me crazy. Besides, I want to listen to the radio."

"You can listen down here," said her father, in a voice that was almost begging. The terrible tension between them was gone now. Amy had lost the awful, cold voice that froze her parents out.

Still she felt sorry for her father. "I don't think you'll like the station I'm going to listen to."

"Why not?" asked her mother. "We're not so old-fashioned. Remember, young lady, I was swooning over Frank Sinatra practically before you were born."

"This isn't Frank Sinatra, Ma. You know that. I've got to listen because I'm sure they're going to play Elvis' new record."

Her father looked as if Amy were making a bad joke.

"It's true," said Amy.

"What's he on, the comedy hour?" asked her father.

Amy didn't answer. She started up the stairs for her room.

"Come on, Amy, can't you take a joke?" asked her father. "Let's listen together."

Amy stood on the stairs, sorry now that

she had mentioned it to her parents, but she felt stuck. She didn't want to start a fight again — that seemed immature. She realized her parents were at least trying.

Her father moved to the radio. "What station?" he asked.

"WHBQ."

Her father gave her a quizzical look. "They play race music, don't they?"

"Dewey Phillips is white, Dad. Everybody knows that."

Dewey Phillips' voice filled the living room.

They listened to a red-hot blues number, the type of music that Elvis loved so much, raw sounds that had never before been heard in the Klinger house.

Amy was uncomfortable, as if she were breaking a taboo, listening to such music with her parents.

Finally at nine-fifteen, Dewey's voice announced that he was going to play a new record by a local boy. Amy found she was so nervous that she was barely breathing. She dug her hands into her lap. It was as if she was going to hear herself on the air.

Then she heard it. It sounded so much like him. It was as if he were right in the room. But different. "That's all right . . . Mama. . . . Di . . . di . . . di. . . . I need your loving . . . that's all right. . . . Any way you do."

His voice reached for high notes, swung up to them. All his humor, all the laughing that seemed behind his eyes . . . all that power, it burst into the living room. Amy felt as if he were breathing for her.

Then it was over, and Dewey was back. Amy started to breath again.

"He sounds just like a nigger," said her mother.

"Shut up," snapped her father. "He's Amy's friend. He's good."

Amy stared at her father. She remembered Elvis' dream. Never in a million years would she have imagined her father telling her mother to shut up. But it had happened. Maybe all their lives were changing.

Her mother put down her needlework. "I never," she said. "Who would have thought that queer-looking boy would be on the radio? Well, at least he was nice enough to call you and let you know he was going to be on the air."

Amy grinned. "Ma, would you like a cracker?" she asked.

Chapter 22

Amy put on a white strapless sundress made of dotted-swiss cotton. It gave her an innocent but sexy look. She looked at herself critically in the mirror. The white of the dress showed off her tan.

She put on a pair of high-heel shoes. She smiled at herself. She liked the way she looked, but she was still nervous. Then she went downstairs to wait.

Tonight was the first time Elvis was performing in public in Memphis. The past month had been crazy for him. Five thousand orders for the record were booked in the first week after it was played on the air. It had been out only three weeks and already it was number three on Memphis' Country and Western chart.

Tonight Elvis was booked into the open-air shell at Overton Park. He had sent over a group of passes. She was going with Carol, Steve, and a group from school. Suddenly all of her friends were telling each other how clever Amy was for knowing that Elvis was special. They asked her to invite him to parties they were giving. Even her mother had taken to asking when he was going to come around again.

"You look beautiful tonight," said her mother, fixing a strand of Amy's hair. "Now I'm sure you're going to be visiting backstage, aren't you? Comb your hair before you go."

"Do you want me to bring him some cheese and crackers for you?"

Her mother looked stunned. "Amy, I'm sorry I said that. Are you going to hold it against me forever?"

Amy shook her head. "No, Ma, I'm sorry. I'm a little nervous tonight about seeing him. I shouldn't have snapped at you."

"You look so beautiful. He's going to be so happy to see you. You'll have a wonderful night."

"Right," said Amy. She kissed her mother on the cheek. "Thanks, Mom. I'm sorry I gave you such a hard time."

Her mother looked flustered. "You're a good girl." Her mother paused. "Well, you're a smart girl, and you've always spoken your mind. I should be used to it. You just go and have a good time."

Amy heard a car horn outside. "That's Steve and Carol. I've got to go." She gave her mother another kiss and then ran out the door.

Carol greeted her with a kiss. Amy had

never seen Carol with so much eye makeup on. She was dressed in a satin sheath dress, and her hair was swept back in a french twist.

"You look like you're going to a formal. It's just an outdoor concert."

"We're going backstage, aren't we?"

"Well, yeah, I guess." Just then the radio began to play Elvis' song, "That's All Right, Mama." Carol danced around on the seat next to Amy. Every time she clapped she missed the beat.

Amy sat with her arms wrapped around her body. The wind from the window was blowing her hair. They parked the car in the lot outside the art museum in Overton Park. The homes surrounding the park were the fanciest in the city.

Amy's heels sunk into the grass as they walked toward the band shell. It was already full of people. Elvis had told her that he had saved her seats up front.

Carol put her arm around Amy's waist as they walked down the steps toward the front of the outdoor arena.

Amy felt someone pull on her skirt. She looked down. Matthew, the bus driver, was grinning up at her.

"I didn't expect to see you here," he said.

Amy shook her head. "Why not?"

"You always seemed like the intellectual type. I would have thought you'd have gone in for classical music."

"Elvis is a friend of mine," said Amy.

"You're kidding," said Matthew. "I just came 'cause I was curious, you know, after hearing his record and knowing that he's local and all that."

Carol tugged at Amy's waist. "Come on, we've got to be going. It's going to start soon," she whispered.

Amy nodded.

"Enjoy the show," she said to Matthew.

Matthew smiled at her. Amy gave him a backward glance as they walked down to the front row.

Elvis was scheduled as the opening act. He had told Amy not to expect too much. "They give the opening act to the guy they think people won't mind missing," he said.

"That's not gonna be true tonight," Amy had told him.

Elvis walked onstage with Scotty and Bill behind him. Nobody had even bothered to introduce him.

Then he kicked off with "That's All Right, Mama." His left leg shook, he swung his head from side to side. His pompadour fell down over his eyes. With every shake of his head, he sent teasing glances out into the audience. Amy thought he was looking right at her.

He just couldn't stand still. He walked up to the lip of the stage. He had the microphone in his hand. He bent it back like it was a girl and he was giving it a soul kiss.

Carol, sitting next to Amy, started to scream at the top of her lungs. The girls around Amy screamed louder. It was as if his leg was an electrode connected to their larynges.

Carol was on her feet, screaming and holding on to Amy's arm. Amy couldn't scream. She could barely breathe. She was crying and laughing at the same time. He was so good!

He ended a song. He looked out at the audience. This time Amy was sure that he was looking at her. She started to weep. Tears streamed down her face.

Carol looked at her. "Are you okay?"

"I'm all right."

Amy rubbed her eyes. She started to clap her hands loudly and then in the next song, she started to scream, just like the other girls.

It seemed just minutes later his set was over.

"Oh, Amy . . . he's just wonderful," swooned Carol when he had finally left the stage.

"He's the same guy you kept telling me was too weird for me," said Amy.

"I was wrong," said Carol.

"Everybody was wrong," said Amy, but she still felt like sobbing, and she didn't know why.

Afterward they went backstage. Elvis was full of sweat. He waved, but he was busy signing autographs, laughing at the girls who surrounded him.

Carol pushed her forward. "Come on," she said. "He wants to talk to you, I bet."

Amy hung back reluctantly.

Scotty saw her and put his arm around her. "What did you think of our boy?" He had a huge grin on his face.

"He was great, and so were you."

"Thanks . . . but he's got something. It drives the girls wild."

Amy glanced over her shoulder. Elvis was deep in conversation with a blond girl who was hanging on every word he said. He looked up and caught Amy staring at him. He winked. Then he turned back to the blond.

Scotty continued to talk to Amy. "We weren't just great. We blew them away," said Scotty. "The other acts are furious." Scotty giggled.

"Congratulations," said Amy, wishing she were somewhere else. Finally, a man grabbed Scotty's arm and dragged him away.

Amy looked over at Elvis and the blond girl. "Maybe we should go," Amy whispered to Carol.

"Are you crazy? You haven't even talked to him yet."

"I think he's got enough to keep him busy," Amy said. But just as she spoke, Elvis broke away. He ambled over. He licked his lips as he got closer. "You get the tickets I sent over?" he asked.

Amy smiled at him. "Right in the front row."

"I saw you," said Elvis, giving her his best

teasing smile, only now it seemed staged to Amy.

Carol poked Amy. "You remember my friend Carol, don't you? And Steve?" Amy took pleasure in pushing Steve forward. "You remember Steve from my party, don't you?"

"Yeah," said Steve. "Listen, I'm sorry for that night."

"Forget it." Elvis put his arm around Amy. "What did you think of the show? I couldn't figure out what the hollering was about." Elvis laughed. "Bill said it was my left leg. It was shaking. I can't help it."

"You were great," whispered Carol. "Really great."

Amy smiled "You were," she said. She watched Elvis. He was trying to be polite, but so many people were grabbing for his attention. She reached up on tiptoe and kissed him on the cheek. "I'll see you."

Elvis looked distracted. "I'm gonna be busy after the show . . . but . . . I'll call you soon."

"Sure," said Amy, turning to leave. She wondered if he was going to be busy with the blond. She saw his mother standing in a corner, glaring at her.

Amy remembered the warning bells that had gone off in her brain the night he had tossed away the words *I love you*. He had mumbled them quickly, as if he wanted to get rid of them. Ever since they had met, Amy was the one who had had to go after him. Now he was moving so fast, she doubted whether she'd ever catch him again.

Chapter 23

Amy held the catalog in her hand. She stood in the registration line. The courses she wanted to take were marked down, but she felt fear in the pit of her stomach that she couldn't remember feeling since kindergarten when she had wet her pants and begged to be taken home.

She had survived kindergarten and eventually taken to school as a refuge from home. It was the one place in her life where she always knew how to perform.

But Humes didn't have some of the college-prep courses she needed, and she had a scholarship to an after-school program at State for "promising high school seniors."

Just being on a college campus felt different. The kids looked so much cleaner and wealthier than the kids at Humes. The boys were wearing jackets and thin ties. The girls were almost all wearing slim skirts, stockings, and cotton blouses with round collars. Amy felt out of place wearing a full skirt with her one horsehair crinoline. She had thought it would give her confidence. Instead, she felt like a little hick kid.

Her mother had offered to go with her, but Amy had insisted on going to registration herself. Now she wished that at least one person she knew was going to State with her.

The line moved slowly. She shifted her weight from one foot to another. Suddenly she heard a voice in her ear whisper, "Ninety-nine bottles of beer on the wall. . . ."

Amy whirled around.

"Matt. . . . What are you doing here?" It was the red-haired bus driver from summer camp.

"I'm taking a college-prep course, too. I didn't realize you were going here."

Amy felt herself blush. She hadn't been very nice to Matt all summer, she realized; never even bothered to find out much about him. Now he turned out to be the only person she knew. Somehow she had just assumed he wasn't very interesting, just because he drove the day-camp bus.

Matt seemed to be reading her mind. "I only took that job to earn money for college."

"Me, too. What are you taking?" So much for clever and striking college kid dialogue, thought Amy.

"Physics, biology. The required stuff. You know — English . . . introduction to European history."

Amy looked down at her catalog. "I'm taking European history, too. And biology

... but not physics. I'm scared of it. But I'm taking an advanced literature course. English is my best subject."

"It's my worst. Maybe you can help me with my papers." Matt kept grinning at her.

Amy realized she was smiling, too. They were having a dumb conversation, but at least they were talking. Why did she feel so comfortable with Matt?

When they both finally made it through the line, Matt asked her if she'd like to have a Coke. They went into the cafeteria, and Amy sat while Matt got them two Cokes.

She sat alone at the table, knowing that if anyone was staring at her, they'd see Matt come back to her. They'd see that she was not alone.

She saw Matt carrying the tray as if he was afraid to spill one drop of it. She leaped up to help him. Their hands touched and Amy jostled the tray, spilling some of the Coke. "Sorry," she mumbled.

"My fault," said Matt.

There was an awkward pause while they sipped their Cokes. Amy couldn't think of anything more to say, but Matt didn't seem bothered by the silence. When they finished he stood up.

"I'll walk you home," he said. Then he blushed. "I just meant . . . if you'd like."

"That would be nice," Amy said. They walked across campus. Amy saw a girl, carrying a huge poster of Elvis into a dorm. It felt like an intrusion from another world.

"That Presley . . . he's something," said Matt.

Amy felt herself bristle. She hoped Matt wasn't going to put Elvis down. Most boys did. They seemed to think Elvis' music was only for girls.

"He is," said Amy noncommittally.

"I think he's terrific," said Matt with a wide grin. "Never heard anything like it. At that concert that I saw you at . . . the one at the outdoor Overton Shell. Girls were practically walking on my head to get up front. I thought I was gonna get killed, but I was screaming, too. He just makes you want to get up and shake."

Amy laughed. "He does. He shakes people up."

Suddenly Matt went into an Elvis imitation, sticking out his leg and shaking it.

Amy stared, thinking, How embarrassing.

Then Mrs. Hunter's face flashed in front of her eyes. What's embarrassing? she asked herself. Asshole. Amy stuck her leg out and started to dance to the imaginary music. Elvis wasn't the only one who could shake people up. Amy didn't care who was watching. She shook her hips and moved her legs, dancing with Matthew to a beat in her head, the beat of life that Elvis had given them all. "All Shook Up."